THE SUMMER OF
LILY & ESME

A NOTE ON THE AUTHOR

John Quinn was born in Co Meath and worked as a teacher before becoming a radio producer in the Education Department of RTE. *The Summer of Lily and Esme* is his first work of fiction and his second children's book, *The Gold Cross of Killadoo,* will be published in 1992.

PRAISE FOR *THE SUMMER OF LILY AND ESME*

"The tone is lyrical and reflective, the narrative compelling and the setting—present and past—evoked with an excellent sense of contemporary detail."

ROBERT DUNBAR, *THE IRISH TIMES*

"A piece of writing breathtaking for its simplicity and sheer readability...highly recommended."

BOOKS IRELAND

THE SUMMER OF
LILY & ESME

JOHN QUINN

POOLBEG

First published 1991 by
Poolbeg Press Ltd
Knocksedan House,
Swords, Co Dublin, Ireland
Reprinted 1992 (twice)

© John Quinn, 1991

The moral right of the author has been asserted.

ISBN 1 85371 208 6

Poolbeg Press receives financial assistance from The Arts Council/An Chomhairle Ealaíon, Dublin

Cover design by Judith O'Dwyer
Set by Richard Parfrey in New Century Schoolbook 12/14.5
Printed by Cox & Wyman Ltd., Reading Berks

For Olive—this time—and to the memory of
Frank Ledwidge, poet and soldier

*And I was wondering in my mind
How many would remember me...*

Contents

1

The Move

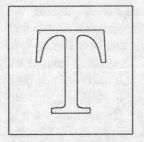hey had spoken very little to him during the journey. A couple of times his father had asked him if the removal van was still following behind. Alan knew that a quick look in the wing mirror would tell his father that the van was indeed following, but he also knew that his father often asked questions just for the sake of asking questions. Never very interesting questions. Just questions. And he always accepted Alan's answers. The answers didn't matter to his father. They didn't matter very much to Alan any more either.

His mother's only remark to Alan was to enquire if he had taken his travel tablet. Yes, he had, even though it was only a forty-minute journey. He would never get sick on a forty-minute journey. He had only got sick once, when they went on a long holiday journey to Kinsale, and even then it was only because of something he had eaten. But that was his mother. Always fussing.

They were nearing the end of the journey now. Tatters seemed to sense it. All during the journey he curled up on the floor at Alan's feet but now he clambered up on the seat beside him and began to look about. They had turned off the main road now, and the narrow winding lane, banked on either side by tall hedges, did not afford much of a view. Occasionally when they passed a gateway Alan caught a fleeting glimpse of the main road they had left, now below, and in the distance the smoky haze that was the city. The city. It had been his home for eleven years. Alan lay back in the rear seat and, running his fingers through Tatters' coat, remembered...

"No 14, Linden Lawn, exceptionally appointed bungalow in quiet cul-de-sac"—that was how the auctioneer had described their former home. Alan had often wondered what exactly "exceptionally appointed" meant. Every time the auctioneer brought someone to see the house Alan had been sent to his room and Tatters had been locked in his kennel. From his room Alan would catch snatches of the auctioneer's patter—

"One of the many outstanding features...has that lived-in feeling but still in immaculate condition..." Immaculate. Of course. Remove your shoes on entering and put on slippers. No friends allowed in the house except on special occasions— birthdays, Christmas. No friends. No friends. No real friends. Never a chance. Tatters was the only real friend. As if he read Alan's thoughts Tatters turned over on his back and stretched his paws out fully. Alan scratched the dog's belly. "The floor, Alan. The dog's place is on the floor." His father spoke to Alan in the mirror. "How many times do I have to tell you?" Alan eased the dog down onto the floor. "We're nearly there now, Alan," his mother added, as if to change the subject. "Watch out for the gateway on the left."

The road seemed to twist and turn all the time now but at last there came a straight stretch. His father flicked the indicator switch and within moments he swung the car through the pillars of the gateway. The gates were no longer there but Alan just had time to notice the words *Glebe House* inscribed in faded black paint on one of the pillars. The rattle of stones leaping up at the underside of the car made Tatters curious and he stood on his hind legs, paws against the door, to see what was happening.

The avenue swept in a gentle arc into a grove of trees which suddenly shut out the sunlight, but in a few moments they were out of the grove and there before them stood Glebe House—a grey two-storey building whose windows glinted in the sunlight.

"Here we are—home sweet home," said his father. "Well, what do you think, Alan?" For once, there was warmth in his question.

"It's—it looks nice."

"It is nice. Wait till you see inside."

All three car doors opened simultaneously but Tatters was out and scurrying around in circles before anybody stood on the gravel drive. Suddenly he froze and gave a low growl. A figure appeared in the doorway of the house. Tatters' growl became an excited bark as he headed for the doorway before Alan called him to heel. The figure came out into the sunlight. It was a small, slightly built woman, dressed in black but also wearing a blue apron.

"Ye're welcome to Glebe House," she called as they approached. Her round face bore a warm smile.

"You'd think she owned the damn place and not us," muttered Alan's father.

"Shush, Michael," his mother muttered from the side of her mouth as she returned the woman's smile. "Thank you, Mrs Grehan. This is my husband, Michael, our son, Alan; and the dog, who was very naughty to bark at you like that, is called Tatters. Mrs Grehan has been cleaning and getting the house ready for us for the last few days."

"Indeed there's little getting ready in it. Just a matter of airing rooms and freshening the place up. But let ye come in. I'll have tea and scones for ye in a minute. Make a wish now as ye cross the threshold of your new home." She led the way into the house. Make a wish, Alan thought. Make a wish. I wish. I wish. Nothing came to mind. A friend maybe. An adventure. "Come on, Alan. Don't you want to see the house?" His mother's voice woke him from his reverie.

It was the size of the rooms that impressed most. Not just the floor space but the height of the ceilings. On either side of the spacious hall were two rooms of equal size, one a dining-room, the other a "drawing-room"—a new word to Alan. Off the drawing-room was a conservatory and from there they looked out on a very large orchard. "I'm afraid the orchard's gone a bit wild." Mrs Grehan spoke their thoughts. "Himself is having a go at it anyway." As if he had heard her, a tall, angular figure appeared from behind an apple tree, swinging a scythe in a slow rhythm. He paused to wipe his brow and turned to wave to the group in the conservatory. "He could do with a mug of tea, obviously," Mrs Grehan laughed.

The bedrooms were equally large. Alan's room was at the back, giving him a better view of the orchard which stretched back in a gentle slope into a huge overgrown hedge. Above the hedge he could just discern the roof of another house in the hazy distance. Civilisation, he thought.

It was as they turned to descend the stairs for Mrs Grehan's tea and scones that Alan noticed the narrow stair that wound up to another floor. Alan went up a few steps and craned his neck to see where the stair led. He was disappointed to find that a huge wardrobe sat at the top. "What's up there?" he asked.

"Oh, that," Mrs Grehan answered quickly. "That's just the attic. There's nothing there but dust and cobwebs. Now are ye going to have the tea and scones?"

"Yes, come on, Alan," his mother added, "you'll only dirty your clothes up there."

Mrs Grehan's scones were delicious, hot and soaking with melted butter. They were all munching away in the kitchen when a shuffling of feet and a stifled cough from the adjoining pantry brought Mrs Grehan to her feet. "Come in, Tom, and don't be so shy!" The tall man they had seen working in the orchard stooped as he entered the kitchen. "This is Mr and Mrs McKay and Alan. This is Old Tom the gardener," she laughed, "and my old husband for forty years." Tom shook hands with all of them. Alan noticed how hard his hand was and how strong his grip. Tom said little until he had gulped down a mug of tea. "Hard work out there?" Alan's father enquired almost diffidently.

"Well, 'tis a long time since that grass fell to a scythe. Tell me—do ye like the house?"

"Yes, yes, we like it very much," Alan's mother replied.

"And what about this young man? Does he like it?"

"Yes I—" Alan began, but Tom interrupted. "'Twill be a big change from the city. Tell us"—he lowered his voice to a whisper—"have ye seen the ghost yet?"

"The ghost?" Alan whispered in reply.

"Yeh, the Glebe ghost. They say it's a boy about your age. People have seen him up at the attic win—"

"Tom Grehan, have you work to do or have you not?" Tom's wife gave him a severe look. Her voice was equally severe. She too lowered her voice in a whisper to Alan. "Pay no heed to that old man's foolish talk." Alan felt both a chill of fear and a thrill of excitement. A ghost. His own age. The momentary silence was broken by the excited yapping of Tatters and the scrunch of tyres on the gravel outside. The removal van had arrived. "Come on," said Mrs Grehan. "There's work for all of us now."

That night Alan lay awake for a long time. He should have been tired. He *was* tired. It had been a long and exciting day. Part of his restlessness was due to the unfamiliar surroundings. He had drawn back the curtains and from his bed he could look out over the fields and trees bathed in bright moonlight. It was the stillness and the absence of artificial light that Alan found most unusual. Back home in the city—no, that wasn't right; this was home—back in the city, the light from street lamps would filter through his curtain, and the night air was punctuated with traffic noises and occasional voices raised in delight or anger. But here it was the stillness; and in that stillness the words of Tom Grehan spun around in Alan's head: a ghost—your own age—attic window—a boy—about your own age.

2
Esme and Lily

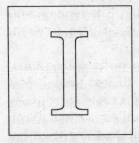t was Tatters' excited barking that woke Alan. He had slept deeply and long. A glance at his watch told him it was ten past ten. It took a few moments for him to become familiar again with his new surroundings. Glebe House. This was his new home. This was his new room. This was—Tatters broke his reverie. He stumbled out of bed and pulled back the curtains. The flood of light drowned him momentarily, but as his eyes became accustomed to the brightness he marvelled at the view before him. Trees and meadows sailed towards him out of a receding mist, as a warm May sun broke through.

Down below, Tatters was yapping away at Tom Grehan. Tom leaned across the crossbar of his bicycle and talked softly to the dog. Tatters sat on his haunches a few yards away and barked back but Tom kept talking as if to a child. Tatters finally relented and crawled forward on his belly until Tom could reach down and gently scratch the dog's head. Tatters had made a friend. Tom was still hunched across the crossbar talking to the dog when Alan's father appeared in his dressing-gown and slippers.

The two men conversed for a few minutes, Tom gesturing towards the house now and then while the younger man nodded earnestly. In one of his gestures Tom pointed towards Alan's window and caught sight of the boy's face. Tom waved cheerily and, as Alan returned the wave, he was disappointed to see Tom mount his bike and head off down the avenue with Tatters frisking along behind him. "Breakfast, Alan," his mother called, "and hurry. We have to get to Mass at eleven."

Mass was in the village of Kildavock, about two miles from Glebe House. Kildavock was a small village, just one street with a supermarket and a few pubs. The church was at the far end of the village. As his father parked the car, Alan was aware of the curious stares of the local people as they hurried in twos and threes into the church. In particular the newcomers came under the gaze of a knot of men at the church gate, men who were in no hurry to go inside. Among them was Tom Grehan, who gave a little salute to the McKay family as they passed by. Kildavock would know all about the newcomers before Mass was over, Alan thought as he dipped his finger in the water font and entered the cool dark of the church.

"No *Sunday Times*!" Alan's father muttered as he slid into the driving seat, tossing a chocolate bar towards Alan in the back. "Had to order the damn thing. The joys of living in the wilds."

"You'll get used to it, dear," his wife answered. "There are compensations. Did you talk to Tom?"

"Yes. He and his sidekick, Mick, will follow us over."

"Oh, good," Alan cried. "Will he be with us all day?" The prospect of having a friend around the house for his first day cheered him. His mother's reply dimmed that cheer quickly. "They're coming to help us with the furniture. Heavy work, not really for boys."

"But I could—"

"You could change out of your good clothes and bring Tatters for a walk."

"And keep him out of our way," his father added. There would be no point in arguing any further. It was Tatters and himself against the world.

Alan changed into a tee-shirt and Bermuda shorts and called Tatters. Although he was disappointed that he could not meet Tom Grehan—and hopefully find out a bit more about the ghost in the attic—it was still nice to get outside.

The day had grown very warm. As he made his way down the orchard he welcomed the shade of the apple trees. There was a glorious scent from the grass Tom had cut, a scent Alan had never experienced before. He lay down on the grass that had fallen to Tom's scythe and tumbled with Tatters, gathering armfuls of the stuff and covering them both in its delicious scent. Tatters soon tired of the game, however, and was off bounding through the uncut grass in the lower part of the orchard. Alan lay where he was, panting from his exertions and brushing the grass from his body. He threw back his head and lay with arms and legs outstretched. The sun was directly overhead, and it was when he shielded his eyes from its glare with his hand that his gaze fell on the little window high up on the back wall of the house. The attic. It must be the attic. And that must be the window where the ghost—the boy—was seen. There was certainly no face there now. In fact the window was distinctly grimy, unlike the other windows, which glinted in the sunlight.

Alan felt the same chill and thrill that had run through him when Tom had first mentioned the ghost. Tom. Maybe if he hung around he might get a word with Tom before he began work. Maybe if he went down the avenue...

Tatters' excited barking interrupted his thoughts. Alan jumped up and it was some time before he could actually catch a glimpse of the dog. The grass was so tall that Tatters had to bound through it in kangaroo hops. Alan laughed at the comical sight of the little black-and-white bundle bobbing up and down. But Tatters had obviously disturbed something and there was a chase on. A rabbit? A hare? Alan gave a whoop and joined in, lunging through the tall grass. He too found it difficult to run and ended up hurdling rather than sprinting, often stumbling and falling over concealed hillocks. He laughed each time he picked himself up, thinking how comical *he* must look. Each time he had to listen for Tatters before he could pick up the trail. The chase took boy, dog and quarry in a crazy zig-zag path which gradually brought them to the bottom of the orchard. Alan paused, breathless from the chase.

A huge wall of brambles, twice his height,

confronted him. Tatters grew even more excited, frustrated by the barrier that allowed his quarry an escape. He ran along the hedge, seeking a way through. And then, in a moment, he was gone. "No, Tatters, no," Alan cried, desperately lunging after the dog towards a small gap in the thicket. The dog had disappeared but Alan's momentum carried him right into the thicket. Instinctively he threw his hands up to protect his face from the brambles. His legs kept going and he landed with a thud on his bottom. Before he had time to recover from the shock of the impact, an amazing thing happened.

Alan careered downwards through the under-growth, lying on his back. His arms flailed as he fought desperately to protect his face. He willed his body to stop but it would not. For a fleeting moment he had a memory of a similar experience—sliding down water rapids at the seaside leisure park. But this was no joyride. As his feet cleared a path, sally rods whipped the rest of his body viciously as if sprung from traps. The brambles were even worse, tearing at his clothes, tangling his hair and lacerating his arms and legs. He fought for his breath, trying to scream, if only in pain, but no sound came from his throat. Once he caught hold of a thick branch, hoping to stop his mad feet-first slide, but the branch snapped and came away in his hand. He shut his eyes tightly for fear of a whipping bramble. His descent seemed almost vertical, plunging him into a hell of torment. His body gained speed as he descended, so much so that it travelled too fast for the whipping rods to hit him, but still the occasional one lashed him, sending a searing pain right through him. The fall seemed as if it would never end, but just when he feared that an even worse fate might await him at the bottom, he shot out into blinding light and landed in a carpet of soft, soft, beautifully soft grass.

The next sensation Alan felt was that of Tatters' warm, moist tongue licking his torn legs. He must have passed out, for how long he did not know. As sensation returned to his body, so did pain. Stinging pain seared through his arms and legs. Blood oozed from a number of red weals which scarred his limbs. His tee-shirt and shorts were badly torn and bits of briar still dangled from both garments. Tatters' attempts to comfort him only seemed to sharpen his pain.

"It's all your fault anyway," Alan whimpered, shoving the dog away from him. The sudden movement of doing so only made him more aware of how sore his whole body was. Tatters slunk away, not understanding the boy's change of mood. Alan slowly eased himself into a sitting position and surveyed his damaged body. He gathered wisps of dry grass and gently wiped his wounds. There was nothing he could do about his clothes. He thought of how his mother would react on seeing him. He winced as he dabbed at a particularly deep gash. He winced even more as he thought of his mother's response. When he had cleaned himself as much as he could, he lay back in the long grass and reflected on his situation. The pain was slowly easing from his body. There remained the problem of making his way back to his own garden. The bramble and thicket wall through which he had plunged looked even more daunting from this side. He was on a much lower level now—so much so that he could not see Glebe House. Yet there was something about his fall that bothered him. Yes, there had been a tangle of briars and under-growth but apart from that the passage through which he slid was quite clear underneath, almost as if...

Alan suddenly became aware of voices in the distance. He listened intently. Above the drone of insects and occasional birdsong, the sound of human voices carried over the drowsy stillness. Alan rolled over and eased himself into a kneeling position. It brought his head and shoulders above the meadow grass. Across the meadow, beyond a low hedge, he could see the back of a two-storey house. This must have been the house whose roof he had noticed from his own window. It wasn't so much the house that attracted his attention now but the voices of two figures who were seated in a clearing just beyond the hedge. Two women, wearing large straw hats.

From a distance he could make out little else but the excited chatter of the pair and the occasional rattle of a tea-cup carried across the hazy meadow. Alan was about to duck down again and make his retreat when Tatters' barking distracted him once again. That dog! Tatters had appeared at the hedge just beside the two figures. There was nothing for it but to retrieve him as quickly as possible. Alan waded across the meadow. An occasional thistle brushed against his legs, reminding him how sore they were. He reached the hedge, called to Tatters in a whisper, grabbed him and swept him into his arms. He didn't dare look across the hedge, and turned to make his escape.

"There you are, Albert. Where ever have you been these last few days?" The voice was frail, and though it seemed to be directed at him, Alan didn't turn around. It couldn't be.

"Yes, Albert, we've been watching out for you

every day, haven't we, Esme?" Another voice, slightly stronger. He turned to face them, the dog still squirming under his arm. They were old, very old. He could barely see their faces under the straw hats. One of the women sat upright in a wheelchair, the other reclined in a sunchair with a walking-stick propped against it.

"I'm—I'm sorry—I'm not—the dog," Alan stuttered.

"Oh, we don't mind Ruffian, do we, Lily?" the woman in the wheelchair replied.

"Just keep him away from Tickles," added Lily.

"Tickles?" queried Alan. "Yes, Tickles—our cat. Really, Albert, you're..."

"Albert!" Esme interrupted her sister. "What on earth happened you?" She peered out from under her hat and began to giggle. "Look, Lily! Albert's fallen down the chute again!"

Lily joined in the giggling. This is crazy, Alan thought. They are crazy. The chute—what did they mean?

"Look, I'm afraid I'm not who you think I am. I'm sorry. I must..."

"So you should be too," said Lily, changing her tone. "You might at least have said if you enjoyed the book."

"Yes," added Esme. "What are we going to tell

Father?"

Father, Alan thought. They were positively ancient. How could their father be...

"Next time he writes from the front he'll say, 'Did Albert enjoy the book?'"

The front? That means a war?

"And we'll say," chimed in Lily, "oh, yes. He loved it so much he never came back for a week!" They were really ganging up on him now.

"No, I didn't," Alan pleaded. "I mean, I wasn't— I'm not—" This was mad. Why am I defending myself? Why can't I explain? I must get out of here.

"Oh, come on, Albert," Esme laughed. "Don't sulk! We're only teasing."

"I'm not sulking," Alan said. "I'm only trying to explain."

"You don't have to explain," Lily reassured him. "We know why. Your father wouldn't let you come. And now you stole out and fell down the chute!"

"Again," added Esme, and they both exploded into giggles once more. This is too much, Alan thought. "I have to go," he blurted. "I'll—I'll come back—soon!" He turned and ran through the meadow, still holding Tatters. He could hear their giggles receding behind him as he ran. He reached the bramble wall, released Tatters and paused for breath. The last hour had been a nightmare. Was it real? Had it happened to him? Maybe it was a case of "Alan in Wonderland?" He managed a smile to himself.

There was still the problem of getting back to his own garden. He crouched, made himself as small as he could and began the painful climb back up the—the chute! This was the chute! But who was Albert? And who were those doddery old women who talked of a father who was still in the war? The questions raced through his mind, now and then clashing with the painful memory of his descent down the chute as he became entangled in another briar. Progress was slow. He slipped back a number of times, colliding with Tatters who struggled behind him. Eventually he made it to the top, stood up with relief, brushed himself off and headed for the house. He was surely for it now. He took a deep breath, opened the back door and stepped inside.

3
Lisa

y God, Alan! What ever happened to...Michael?" His mother turned away to summon her husband. "What did you do to yourself?"

"I only fell into—"

She didn't give Alan time to finish the sentence but called even more urgently to her husband. Her voice broke into a sob.

"It's all right, Mum. I only fell into some briars. I'm not really hurt," Alan pleaded. His father appeared in the doorway with Tom Grehan behind him.

"Oh, Michael. Look at the state of him!" His mother was crying openly now. "Get a doctor, quick!"

"For God's sake, Deirdre. There's no need to panic. He's still standing! He's still breathing!

Here, let's have a proper look at you." His father guided Alan to the kitchen window. "There you are! Just a few scratches! Now, young man. Perhaps you can explain to us how you got into this state?"

"Never mind how he got into it. He needs treatment!" Alan's mother was approaching hysteria.

"He's not going to die, Deirdre, and before he gets cleaned up I want to know where's he's been and what he's been at. Now, calm down!" His father stared firmly at his mother and at the same time spoke to his son. "I'm waiting, Alan..."

There was a momentary silence before Tom Grehan interrupted. "Sure he was just dragged through a hedge backwards, that's all." Alan stole a glance at Tom and noticed the glint in his eye. Tom's words had at once broken the tension and eased Alan's embarrassment at Tom seeing him in this state. If only Tom knew how close to the truth he was, Alan thought.

"Well, sort of," he blurted. "I was down the garden. It's—it's very overgrown down there—and Tatters—well, he found a—rabbit or something and gave chase. So I chased him." The words were coming easily now but he would have to be careful. "He ran into a clump of briars and I—I couldn't stop myself and fell down—down into them. I—I tore myself more getting out than I did falling in!" He swallowed quickly and waited. It was near enough to the truth, anyway.

Again Tom came to his rescue. "I should have warned ye about the orchard all right. Hasn't been touched for years. Parts of it are like the jungle. I'll have a go at it tomorrow evening!" As his parents turned to Alan, Tom winked at him. It was almost as if Tom knew the whole story. Alan smiled back. He had known this man for less than a day and yet he felt more like a lifelong friend. Alan wished he could throw his arms around Tom's broad but slightly stooping shoulders. Instead he tried to convey his thanks in the warmth of his smile.

"I don't know," his father said, studying Alan's tattered clothes. "If you ask me there's more to it than that, but I'll take you at your word, Tom." He'd take Tom's word but he wouldn't take mine, Alan thought. "And as for you, sir— bed!"

"But I don't need to go to bed. I've only got a few scratches and I'm—"

"Bed, sir!" His father's voice was like that of an army officer. Alan gave a pleading look towards his mother.

"It's best," she said. "You've had a shock and I'll bring you up some nice lunch. Now where did I put the medicine box? We'll have to see about those cuts." She busied herself opening and closing the doors of the kitchen presses, leaving Alan uneasy in the presence of his father. Tom had shuffled down the hall, whistling nervously to himself. His father stood there waiting for his command to be obeyed. Alan turned quickly and dashed down the hall. Tom was standing in the open front doorway surveying the sky and announcing to no-one in particular, "I think we'll have a bit of a splash before long."

Alan paused at the foot of the stairs. "Tom," he called softly. The stooped shoulders turned round. There was so much Alan wanted to say to the man but only one word would come. "Th-Thanks." He turned away, embarrassed at having to retreat to bed. Tom smiled, shook his head upward and gave the knowing wink that Alan had come to appreciate in such a short time. His heart lightened, he bounded up the stairs three at a time. "Yes, he says," Tom spoke out again, addressing no-one in particular, "I think we'll have a bit of a splash before long. There's an unnatural heat about." Alan smiled. There was something peculiar about the way Tom had uttered that last sentence.

Tom was of course right. Within an hour the heaviness of the day had given way to a tremendous downpour, with the occasional rumble of thunder in the distance. It was more than "a bit of a splash..." Alan sat on his bed, propped up by pillows, watching the rain trace crazy patterns on the window. His arms and legs still smarted where his mother had applied liquid antiseptic. The occasional stab of pain reminded him of that pain's origins. The maze of rivulets careering and crossing down the window-pane became the nightmare tunnel through which he had fallen. Automatically he threw his hands up again to protect his face. No, not the tunnel. The chute.

"Look, Lily! Albert's fallen down the chute again!" He could hear them both giggling. The rivulets of rain danced to their giggles. Lily and— what was the other name? A funny-sounding name. Esme. That was it. Lily and Esme. He strained to peer through the window and catch a glimpse of the old women's house but he could see no further than the orchard.

Lily and Esme. Their giggles trailed away in an echo. Who were they? They seemed to know him, or at least they knew someone like him. Someone called Albert. This is the limit, Alan thought. We move to a new house in the country.

I have the whole summer holidays before me and the only neighbours I can find are two ancient women who think I'm someone else! And yet he couldn't banish them from his thoughts. He wasn't offended by their giggles. He smiled as he pictured the broad sun-hats flopping up and down to their chuckles. He suddenly became anxious about their well-being as the rain drummed even more heavily. Had they got in out of the rain in time? Who looked after them—or did they live alone? Of course someone looked after them. It wasn't his problem. He remembered his parting words to them. "I'll be back—soon." Did he say that just to get away or—did he really mean it?

The sound of the car starting up and moving across the gravel woke Alan from his reverie. He rushed to the landing to see his father at the wheel and the figure of another man in the passenger seat. Probably Tom. He turned away to see another figure begin a difficult ascent of the stairs, struggling sideways with a large cardboard box. The man's head was hidden by the box, but there was no mistaking the stoop of the shoulders. "Tom!" Alan cried with delight. "I thought you had gone!"

The answer came in a series of grunts as man and box wrestled their way up the stairs. "No!

'Twas Mick. Had to go. Has a—sick calf—at home..." He paused a few steps from the top. "And a missus—who doesn't like eatin' dinner—on her own!" He gave one more lunge, slid the box onto the landing and flopped down on the window-ledge beside Alan. "That box will be the death of the ould back! Tell me," he drew a deep breath, "how is every bit of you?"

Alan was amused at the expression. "Every bit of me is fine," he laughed. "But some bits are better than others." Their conversation was interrupted by the excited yapping of Tatters who had recognised Alan's voice and came clambering up the stairs. He sprang from the top step in between boy and man and nuzzled against Alan. It was a warm feeling. The three of them huddled on the window-ledge, Tom with his long legs stretched against the box he had parked on the landing. The cosiness of the situation gave Alan confidence. "Tom," he looked out at the rain and paused for a moment, "the house across the fields, at the back. Who—?"

"So that's where you were!"

"I didn't say I was there," Alan retorted sharply. "I just wondered who lived there!" When he turned to look Tom straight in the face, he realised he had offended the man. "I—I'm sorry," he said, sheepishly directing his attention to

Tatters.

"That's the twins you met," Tom replied.

"The twins?"

"Mmm. The Thompson twins."

Alan stifled a giggle. He was tempted to make a joke about ancient pop-singers but he reckoned that Tom might not be into the pop scene. He misjudged the man.

"Now you know why they haven't been in the charts recently," he chuckled, adding by way of explanation, "I have grandchildren who keep me informed on these things." He changed his tone. "Ah, God love them, they're a harmless pair of old dears. Been in that house all their lives."

"But they knew me—or at least they confused me with someone else."

"Sure they've been confused for years. They're not really with it, as you might say. Did you not meet Mrs Bradley?"

"No. I wasn't there very long," Alan explained.

"Well, if you go back watch out for her. She looks after the twins." There was doubt in his voice. "And she's what you might call a sharp woman. Tell us, how did you come across them?"

Alan explained how he had fallen down the chute. "You see," he went on, "the twins called it that. The chute. They knew about it."

"That's a curious one, all right." Tom looked

genuinely puzzled. "I'll have a look at it tomorrow when I tackle the lower orchard."

"Maybe you'll help me hack away the briars," Alan suggested. "I don't want to fall down there again."

"Maybe," said Tom. He had a faraway look in his eye. There was a pause in their conversation. Alan was quite content to sit there, ruffling Tatters' coat. He felt completely at ease in this man's company. If only, he thought. If only...

The quiet was broken by the sound of an approaching car. Tom rose awkwardly from his low-seated position. "Time to move," he said, "or I'll get the sack and you'll get into more trouble! Back to your room. Ach! The ould bones are getting very stiff."

As he rose, Alan found himself facing the stairs to the attic. The ghost! He had forgotten all about the ghost! "Tom," he cried. "The ghost. I meant to ask you—"

"That's a story for another day," said Tom, stooping over the box before staggering with it into a front bedroom.

"But, Tom—" the boy pleaded.

Tom was whistling to himself, and below, the car door opened and shut. It was time for Alan to retreat to his room.

The sound of voices coming from the kitchen woke him. He must have dozed off. His mother's voice was calling, "Alan! Are you there? Come on down. There's someone here to see you."

Someone to see him? Who? He didn't know anyone around here. Anyway he was reluctant to appear before strangers in his present state.

His mother insisted. "Come on. We're waiting!"

He shuffled nervously into the kitchen.

"Glory be to God but you're a sight to behold!" Mrs Grehan cried in surprise. Alan was relieved that it was only Mrs Grehan, but his relief was short-lived. "Look who we have for you," Mrs Grehan went on. In a darkened corner behind him Alan had not noticed another figure. "This is my granddaughter, Lisa. She'll be staying with us for the summer, so ye'll be seeing lots of each other! Lisa's the same age as yourself, Alan, so ye'll have plenty in common."

Lisa emerged into the light. She was as tall as himself, her hair swept back in a ponytail from a bright face that wore a nervous smile. She raised a hand in greeting. He returned the gesture and added a weak "Hi!"

There was an awkward silence. "A pity 'tis still raining," said Mrs Grehan. "Ye could have gone for a walk—to see the sights of Kildavock," she added with a giggle.

"The television's working—in the drawing-room," Alan's mother suggested. The two young people took the hint. The television screen offered a focus to distract their attention from each other. Alan felt distinctly uneasy. He wasn't used to the idea of a friend, but the idea of a girl as a friend was totally new to him. It frightened him. Lisa suddenly began to giggle.

"What's so funny?" Alan asked.

"You," she laughed. "You look like someone who was dragged through a hedge backwards!"

"That's exactly what your grandad said," Alan snapped. "And anyway I was!" he added sheepishly. He stole a quick look at the girl. They both began to giggle. The giggles grew into open laughter. The ice was broken. Conversation came easily as Alan explained his cuts and scratches. For now he said nothing about Lily and Esme. They exchanged views on school, on parents and on Lisa's grandparents. They had both finished school for the year—Lisa because her class had gone for a week to France, Alan because of moving house. Lisa was the second-eldest of a family of five and lived in County Wexford. She loved coming to stay with her grandparents.

"Don't you get bored?" Alan asked.

"No. There's always something to do. Always something happening. You'd be surprised!"

"I will," Alan laughed. "I will."

"And anyway, living with grandparents is cool! There's never any hassle!"

Alan couldn't comment on that. He had a grandfather—his father's father—somewhere in South Africa but there was never any communication from him. The rest of his grandparents were dead. He had warm memories of one—his mother's mother—but she had died three years ago. Tatters had been her dog and he was her legacy to Alan.

"Talk of the devil—here he comes!" Lisa's voice interrupted his thoughts. A red van had pulled up outside. Tom Grehan got out and Lisa ran to the window to wave to him. He had come to collect Lisa and Mrs Grehan. Lisa clambered into the back of the van and made a funny face at Alan through the little window in the back door. Alan smiled. "See you!" he called.

As he stood there Tom ambled past him, and before he opened the driver's door, he turned to the boy. "I've just remembered something else," he whispered. "The ghost—he's supposed to be a boy called Albert!" The name seemed to pierce Alan's head. Albert! *"Look, Lily, Albert's fallen down the chute again!"* Alan was momentarily dazed. By the time he had come to, the red van was turning the bend in the avenue, through the little grove, and he could just discern a smiling face pressed against the back window and the driver's long arm waving him goodbye.

4

The Chute

lan's mind was in a flurry. Albert, the ghost. Albert at the window. *"Look, Lily, Albert's fallen down the chute again!"* There was no doubt now. Whether he wanted to or not, he would have to see Lily and Esme again. He would have to enter their world in order to find out more about Albert. He would have to pretend to be Albert. It wasn't a question of humouring the two women. To them he *was* Albert, anyway.

Next morning his father left early for work. He had a much longer journey to the office now so there would be an early start every morning. Punctuality was very important to Michael McKay, but today there was an added reason for his early departure, as Alan discovered during a lingering breakfast with his mother. "Guess what?" she chirped with delight. "I'm getting a car today! Not new but a very good second-hand one. Dad's gone in to organise it. The garage is sending it out later. It means I can go shopping in Newbridge, go visiting, go—wherever I want!" She was like a child who had been promised a long-sought toy. He was pleased for her. "But don't think I'll be a taxi service! You have your bike and you and Lisa can go exploring on bikes—as long as you're careful on the roads."

"Oh, Mum, I only met Lisa yesterday. It doesn't mean we're going to go everywhere together."

"No, but you got on well together and—" she paused, changing her tone, "you need company." He said nothing but played a game of "battleships" with the few remaining cornflakes floating in the bottom of his cereal bowl.

"Mum," he said casually, "do you remember when Gran—before she died—did she go kind of funny?"

"What ever do you mean?" His mother was quite startled by the question.

"Well, did she—know you or did she forget who you were?"

"Oh, she knew me all right," his mother laughed. "Kept giving me instructions and complaining about the food. Except for the last few days, when her mind wandered a bit—" She stopped herself short. "Alan, why on earth are you asking me this?"

"Oh, nothing," he said, trying to sound casual. "Just wondering." The "battleships" had all sunk without trace.

"Really, you come out with the strangest things at times, Alan. Have you been reading some odd book?"

"No, Mum," Alan said resignedly.

"Well, there's work to be done and I need help," his mother added briskly. "Put your jeans on and an old shirt. I don't want those cuts opening up again."

"Yes, Mum," Alan sighed. The real Mum had returned.

About midday two cars arrived. It was the men from the garage. One was a mechanic in overalls driving a smart-looking blue Fiesta. His mother's car. The other man wore a suit. The salesman. He proceeded to point out the many "excellent features" of the Fiesta. He reminded Alan of the auctioneer who had sold their house. The mechanic got into the second car and switched on the radio to full volume, jerking to the beat of the music that blared out and drumming his fingers on the steering wheel. His mother reverted to the excited state she had been in at breakfast. "Alan, Mr Reilly's bringing me for a test drive. Won't be long. Will you be all right on your own?" She didn't wait for an answer but hopped into the driving seat, impatient to get away. Alan waved goodbye. The mechanic had reclined his seat and lay back, drinking in the music. Alan smiled and went back into the house. He made his way up the stairs and was about to turn into his room when again the attic stairs attracted his attention.

The stairs were very narrow, less than half the width of the main stairs and curving as they went. Even in the bright midday the top of the stairs was quite dark. Alan looked for a light-switch but there was none. He felt his way along the curving wall, counting the steps as he went. Twelve and then a small landing. The big wardrobe loomed in front of him. It was locked. He searched hopefully along the top for a rusting key covered in dust, and smiled to himself when the search proved fruitless. That only happens in "Famous Five" stories, he thought. He put his shoulder against a corner of the wardrobe and shoved until it cut into his shoulder-blade. It wouldn't budge. He tried from the other side. Nothing. He knew that it wasn't the size of the wardrobe that was defeating him. He felt that the wardrobe was secured in some other way. It

was bolted either to the floor or the wall. His
eyes had now grown accustomed to the poor
light. He moved back to the edge of the landing
and, standing on tiptoes, he could just make out
the top of a door-frame behind the wardrobe. He
felt a strange surge within him. He would have
to get beyond that door. Somehow, impossible
though it seemed, he would find a way into the
attic room. But not now. His mother had
returned.

The afternoon passed quickly, largely because
of his mother's good humour. She had liked the
car and had taken it. She moved airily from one
task to another, often humming to herself or
passing a humorous comment to Alan. She really
is like a child at Christmas, he thought.

There was a lot of unpacking to be done, and
between them they made good progress. Alan
kept an eye out for Tom Grehan when he could.
His mind was never far from Lily and Esme, the
chute, the attic, Albert. He gave a little jump of
delight when at last the familiar red van drew
up outside. He watched as Tom produced an
amazing selection of implements from the back
of the van: scythe, axe, hatchet, clippers and a
variety of vicious-looking hooks. "Can I go with
Tom?" he asked excitedly.

"Well," his mother drawled, "we've done well in here and you need the air. But stay away from the briars! And don't get in Tom's way!"

"Yes, Mum." He was already at the back door.

"And put on your wellies! The grass is still very wet."

Alan growled to himself as he rooted in the back porch for his wellingtons. Mother would never wander too far from being Mother, he thought as he hopped down the path on one leg, pulling a wellington with some difficulty onto the other.

Tom was in the lower orchard sorting out his weapons. "War has been declared on the jungle," he announced, as he surveyed the near-wilderness before him. "It's just a matter of deciding where to launch the first attack! Maybe a surprise stab at this clump of briars here. The grass? No. The grass is too wet. Or maybe," he winked at Alan, nodding backwards at the overgrown hedge behind him, "a major assault on our friend here! He's watching my every move."

Before Alan could reply, Tom had pounced on a long-handled hook and turned to advance on the hedge. He swept the hook in a mighty arc and lopped a straggling branch that was foolish enough to challenge him. "Aah! The slash-hook is the only man for these boyos!" Alan was amazed at the strength of the man and at his agility. He seemed to concentrate on particularly stout branches. Each time one of those fell to the slash-hook, Tom took up a small axe and began trimming the branch.

"Tom."

"Yeh?"

"You haven't forgotten the chute?"

"The chute?"

"You know—where I fell down."

"Oh, yeh." Tom laid another trimmed branch on a neat pile.

Alan was growing frustrated. "Well?"

"We must see about that, all right."

"And Albert?"

"Albert?"

"Ah, Tom, come on. You told me last night—"

Tom exploded into laughter. "Am I givin' you a hard time?"

"Yes." Alan poked, embarrassed, at the branch-trimmings.

"Well, all I know is his name was Albert. Something tragic happened to him. And it's got something to do with that window."

"But—"

"That's all I know. Now, we have work to do!"

The work was the clearing of the chute. Again

displaying great agility for a man of his size, Tom wormed his way down the chute armed with a smaller hook and a clippers. He lay on his back, his legs propped against saplings which held his weight, and carved a tunnel above and beside him. He then lowered himself further down the chute and repeated the exercise. When he had cleared a few feet of passageway in this manner, he called to Alan. "Throw me one of those poles I trimmed!" Alan slid a pole down to him. Tom turned onto his belly and laid the pole across the chute, trapping it on either side against the strong saplings and undergrowth. When the pole was secure he grabbed with both hands and pulled. It barely moved. "Good!" Tom muttered to himself. Alan was puzzled until Tom called for a second pole when he had tunnelled another few feet down. He positioned this pole in the same way as the first, and once again he tested it with his full weight.

"That's really clever," Alan called down. "It's like a giant ladder."

"Aye. A dual-purpose ladder," Tom grunted as he hacked away. "It'll stop you flying down at fifty miles an hour, tearing yourself and your clothes to bits." He turned on his belly once more. "And you'll find it very handy when you want to climb back up!"

"You're a genius, Tom," Alan shouted as Tom moved further down the chute.

"Not quite. If I was a genius I wouldn't be down here on my back cuttin' briars!" He paused for a rest. "I was never any good at the books. Old Master Sweeney was right! 'Grehan,' he would say, 'I can see you landing a big job in the bank—the turf-bank!' Aye! God be with the dead. Did you ever see a turf-bank, Alan?"

"No."

"Well, you'll have to come with us to the bog next week and we'll make a turf-man out of you. Now throw me down another pole till we finish this. If your mother comes down here and finds me burrowing like a rabbit we're all done for!"

Alan laughed at the prospect. They were like two pals of the same age. While he valued the older man's wisdom (and strength—he could never have imagined himself clearing the chute like this)—they were totally at ease in each other's company. The "we" convinced Alan of this. With Tom's strength and speed the clearance took less than an hour. Tom clambered back up the chute, pausing occasionally to trim back a briar here and there and using up the surplus poles by reinforcing some rungs of the "ladder" with a second pole. "There," he sighed as he stood erect and brushed the clay and sprigs of briar from his clothes, "what do you think of that?"

"It's brilliant," Alan said. "It's a perfect tunnel!"

"I should have got a job digging the Channel Tunnel," laughed Tom. His voice changed in tone. "You were right, by the way. You weren't the first to go down that tunnel—chute," he added, deep in thought. There was a silence between them. Neither dared to speak out his thoughts. "Well," said Tom finally, "are you not going to try it out?"

Mindful of his last trip down the chute, Alan made his way gingerly this time, but Tom's ladder worked perfectly. Each rung held firm and not a briar interfered with his passage. He made his way through the meadow following the track he had made himself a few days previously. There were no voices to be heard this time. As he neared the hedge, he dropped on all fours and crept forward. He peered through the privet. There was no-one on the lawn. Alan felt an acute disappointment. He had been looking forward, for a number of reasons, to meeting Lily and Esme again. One of the reasons was his genuine concern for them. Maybe one— or both—were unwell. He crept across the lawn to the shelter of a huge ash tree whose branches drooped to within a couple of feet of the ground.

He watched from behind the broad trunk of the tree.

There was little sign of movement in the house. Once he caught sight of a figure moving between rooms. It was neither Lily nor Esme. A voice called within the house but Alan could not discern what was said. His attention was suddenly distracted by the excited yapping of Tatters, whose head bobbed up and down as he bounded across the meadow. "No, Tatters, no!" Alan whispered to himself. The dog burrowed through the hedge and made for the tree. Alan did his best to stifle the barking but the dog would not be restrained. He whimpered and danced to show his excitement at having located his master. Alan made another vain dive to arrest the dog and found himself at the feet of a tall woman dressed in black. From his position lying on the ground she seemed to tower into the tree above. "Well, young sir." Her voice was cold and thin. "And what might you be doing here?" Alan got to his knees and then to his feet. He was too ashamed to look her in the face but stole a quick glance before turning away. Her face was angular and drawn. This must be Mrs Bradley, he thought. What was the word Tom had used to describe her? Sharp. It seemed to describe both her features and her manner.

"Well?" she squeaked impatiently.

"I...I came looking for...for my dog." He pointed to Tatters, who now sat with paws outstretched, panting after his exertions.

"I would have thought the opposite," she said, unimpressed. "And where would you have come from?"

"From Glebe House. We moved there at the weekend." He felt that this would soften her attitude.

"Oh! We have new neighbours." Her voice grew colder, if anything. "Well, you've found your dog." The suggestion was obvious. He gathered Tatters into his arms and turned to go. He steeled himself. "Would you tell Lily and Esme I was here."

"How do you know their names? You're new here." She advanced towards him. He had walked into a trap of his own making, but he felt strangely emboldened. "I...I met them the other day when...when I was trying to catch my d—" He realised how stupid his excuse sounded the second time around, even if it was the truth this time.

"It seems you spend most of your time chasing that creature," she sneered.

"Are they all right?" he asked, ignoring her remark.

"Of course they are all right," she snapped. "Why wouldn't they be?"

"I...I just wondered," he answered lamely. Then, bold again, he asked, "Is it all right to come and see them?" He paused. "Sometimes?"

"I don't see what interest a boy your age could have in two 82-year-old women."

"They were just—friendly."

She spoke no more but waited for him to go. He stepped through a gap in the privet hedge and released Tatters into the meadow. He took a few paces and turned. The woman in black had not moved. "Tell them," he called, "tell them Al—" he checked, "Albert...tell them Albert was asking for them." She said nothing. Alan turned to follow his path through the meadow. It had been a scary experience, but he found himself smiling.

5
Jane

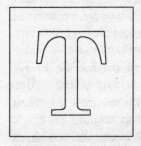

om wasn't visible when Alan climbed back up the chute but there was evidence of his work directly in front of the boy. A huge mound of briars and branch-trimmings had been built up just at the entrance to the chute. "Clever," Alan thought as he looked around for his friend. Voices came to him from further up the orchard.

"There you are, Alan," his mother called. "We were wondering where you had disappeared to."

"I was just...exploring," Alan replied uneasily.

"This is Mrs Patterson—the rector's wife. She came to welcome us to the area." Alan shook hands with the woman who sat at an angle, facing his mother, on the garden seat. She was tall and fresh-faced. Her blonde hair enveloped a warm and winning smile. What struck Alan

most about her was her youth. She was, if
anything, younger than his mother. To Alan the
word "rector" suggested an old man. Since he
had never met a rector he had no reason to
expect this, but that was the image he had.
Consequently a rector's wife should be middle-
aged at least. He felt awkward in her presence.
"You can entertain Mrs Patterson for a while,
Alan," his mother interjected, adding to his
awkwardness. "I'll get us a cup of tea." Alan
shuffled nervously, poking one foot at some
imagined movement in the grass.

"Sit down and tell me what you think of
living in the country. And the name is Jane," the
blonde woman laughed. Her voice was soft with
a hint of a Northern accent.

"It's OK—so far."

"We're only here two years ourselves. It's
quiet—a lot quieter than Derry—but we like it.
And do you like the house?"

"Mmm!"

"Of course, I've been telling your mum it's our
house you're living in."

"What…what do you mean?" Alan was startled
by her remark.

"That was a joke, Alan! You see this house—
Glebe House—used to be the rector's house in
days gone by—the good old days!" she laughed.

Alan's sudden interest in this revelation dissolved his embarrassment immediately. "You mean—rectors used to live here? When?"

"Oh, for donkeys' years. At least when they had a decent congregation. Poor Stephen spends his Sundays dashing about four parishes."

"But when...how long did rectors live here?" Alan was more interested in the past than in her husband's present difficulty.

"Let me see. Old Rev Grimshaw moved out of here—mmm—must be ten years ago. Then Rev Hopkins built the bungalow. And then—us!"

"But how far back does it go?"

"My, but you have a great interest in church history!" she laughed. "Oh, I don't know. Must go back to the last century. You should talk to Stephen. He has all the parish records."

Alan was silent. Here was a key to the past. To the mystery of Albert. If Albert lived in Glebe House seventy years ago, his father must have been a rector. And Stephen—Mr Patterson—had the records...

"Now here we are!" His mother had arrived with a tray. "Are you joining us for tea, Alan?"

"N-no, thanks."

"Well, there's an orange drink in the fridge, if you're—"

"Oh, good, I'll have that!"

"Please?"

"Please!"

"See you, Alan," Jane called after him.

"Yes. See you!"

"You know, Deirdre, you have a real history scholar there..." he heard Jane Patterson remark as he entered the house.

Over the next few days Alan kept a look-out for Lily and Esme, but as he scanned their garden from the bottom of the chute there was no sign of movement. Alan was disappointed. He felt that Mrs Bradley was deliberately imprisoning the sisters in their house. He had no evidence of this, other than their absence from the garden, but Mrs Bradley's attitude to him had left him with feelings of unease. He decided to discuss the matter of Lily and Esme with Lisa when she came to visit.

"Those old dears," was Lisa's first reaction. "Everyone says they're dotty."

"They may be...confused, but they're very friendly."

"But you've only met them once!"

"Once was enough. I...I liked them. They're probably just...just lonely." His spirited defence of the sisters surprised Lisa. She fell silent.

"Do you know anything about Mrs Bradley?"

he enquired.

"Bit of a witch! She's been with them for years. Must be nearly as old as they are," she mumbled as she munched an apple.

"Not really! They're eighty-two. She told me," he added quickly, seeing her surprise as she stopped in mid-bite of the apple.

Alan's frustration at not seeing the twins had reached its limit. He doubted if Mrs Bradley would let him into the house, but he resolved to knock on their front door if there was no sign of them on the following day. There was no need for the bold approach. His heart leaped the next afternoon when he saw the familiar figures through the heat haze across the meadow. He started running. He had left Tatters asleep under the kitchen table where the dog had sought to escape the day's oppressive heat. Alan found himself panting for breath when he reached the far side of the meadow. The sisters had their backs to him so this time he would have the element of surprise. He paused. "Let's see," he thought. "Esme in the wheelchair, Lily with the stick. That's it!" He repeated the identification formula a couple of times before stepping through the privet hedge.

"Hello, Esme! Hello, Lily!" he said cheerily, as if he had known the sisters all his life. The women were somewhat startled until Alan came around into their view.

"Oh, it's you," Esme said diffidently. Alan was hurt by her attitude. "We were just talking about you, weren't we, Lily?"

"Mmm," Lily replied, drawing a needle through an embroidery pattern.

Alan noticed that the thread totally missed the pattern and seemed to wander haphazardly around the pattern sheet. "We thought you had left the country. Gone to beat the Germans all on your own," Esme added, before starting to giggle helplessly. Lily joined in the giggling. Alan became defensive.

"I—I was busy. And anyway I did come and you weren't here. Mrs Bradley told me—"

"Oh, don't mind old Badger. You're not afraid of her, are you, Albert?" Esme spluttered. Alan felt reassured both by being called "Albert" again and by their attitude to Mrs Bradley. "Badger" was just perfect. He smiled.

"Look, Lily. Albert's smiling!" She began to sing a fragment of a song: "Hap-py days are here a-gain."

Lily clapped hands to the beat. "You should smile more often, Albert. It suits you. Esme's always saying that!"

Alan felt himself blushing. Maybe I don't smile

enough, he thought, but they're talking about Albert, not me.

"Anyway, Mrs...anyway, Badger said"—he relished the word—"that I couldn't come into the house. And you weren't out here, so—"

"It's all right, Albert," Esme broke in impatiently. "You don't have to explain *everything*."

"Badger's so fussy," Lily added. "I do wish Mother would hurry up and get better."

Now we're getting into things, Alan thought. He seated himself on the grass, throwing a quick glance at the kitchen window. The severe face of "Badger" peered out at him. He ignored her, propping himself up on one elbow.

"How is your mother now?" Alan asked casually, plucking at a daisy.

"Badger says she will be in hospital for quite a while."

"It takes a broken leg quite a while to mend, you know," Esme added, doing her best to mimic Badger's sharp voice. Alan laughed. He plucked several more daisies. "She must have had a bad fall?" he suggested, holding his breath.

"Horrendous," Lily answered. "That's how your mother described it." Alan was uneasy. He looked around for more daisies. He was on dangerous ground now. He knew little of his "mother"—yet. Esme came to his aid.

"I feel sorry for poor Beauty. That was the first time she ever fell."

"And I was so looking forward to riding her," Lily continued. "Mother promised us both we could have a ride on Beauty for our tenth birthday."

The pieces of the jigsaw were starting to fall into place. Esme suddenly burst into tears. "And now Beauty's dead," she sobbed, "and Mother's in hospital. They probably won't even let her out for our birthday."

"And Badger says we can't visit her there." Lily's voice was trembling.

Alan found himself choking back a tremor in his own voice. He felt so sorry for the two old ladies. Strangely, it was only when they cried that they seemed "old." When they giggled and poked fun at him he accepted them totally as young girls.

"We'll think of something," he said, splicing the daisy stems with his thumbnail. "Anyway," he added boldly, "your birthday's not for a while yet."

"It's on the fifth of August, Albert Dixon," Esme said, brightening up. "And you had better not forget it! We'll be expecting a big present, won't we, Lily?"

"Mmm," said Lily, intent on her embroidery

again.

Albert Dixon. Another clue. The parish records. He hastily threaded each daisy through a splice.

"After all," Lily paused at her embroidery, "Father went to a lot of trouble to get our present for you."

"Sent it all the way from the front," Esme boasted; "even got Mr Ledwidge to sign it for him."

Mr Ledwidge? Alan racked his brain desperately. The name meant nothing to him.

"Father says Mr Ledwidge is going to be Ireland's greatest poet." Lily was looking directly at Alan. "He says when the war is over he's going to bring Mr Ledwidge to meet us!"

"So there!" chirped Esme. "And you haven't even read his book yet."

"I have! I have!" Alan lied. "I'll read some of his poems for you—soon."

This is always what happens with a jigsaw, he thought. You get off to a great start with one corner and then—blank! Nothing seems to fit.

"I wish the silly old war would end soon," Esme sighed. "We haven't seen Father for nearly a year."

"Since the Inniskillings went to France," Lily added. "I hate France. Horrible place. Have you ever been to France, Albert?"

"Yes...no! I mean, no—I haven't. Yes—it is a horrible place," he added weakly. Yes, Alan had been to the south of France for two weeks two years ago, but no, Albert had never been there. And yes, it was a horrible holiday...

"Here you are. An early birthday present for each of you!" He held up two daisy-chains triumphantly.

"Oh, how lovely!" Esme was genuinely pleased. "We must put them on at once."

He helped Esme remove her floppy sun-hat and dropped the daisy-chain over her head. Lily was already arranging hers as if it were a diamond necklace.

"Thank you, Albert. You are very kind."

The sisters sat there admiring their presents.

"I definitely think mine's got more daisies than yours, Lily!"

"No, no," Alan laughed. "They're both exactly the same. I counted!"

There was silence. The hum of insects. A car passing on a distant road. An occasional chirp from a bird in the hedgerow. It was very pleasant to be in the sisters' company. Alan lay back and looked up at the sky. Only a tiny puff of cloud broke the startling blue.

"Did you ever wish you could ride on a cloud and sail all over the world?" he asked dreamily.

"Think of all the places you could go!"

"I'd go to Samarkand," said Esme excitedly.

"Samarkand?"

"Yes. It's a place far, far away—in India or somewhere. It was in one of Mr Kipling's stories that Father read to me. Where would you go, Albert?"

"I'd go to Australia, as long as I didn't fall off!"

Esme laughed, but Lily was strangely silent.

"What about you, Lily?" Alan enquired.

Lily fingered her daisy-chain and looked across the meadow. "I'd like to go to France," she said slowly, "to see what it's really like."

Another silence fell on the three, an uneasy silence. It was suddenly broken.

"What's the meaning of this? Do you want these ladies to get sunstroke?" For the second time Alan found himself looking at Mrs Bradley from grass level, as she replaced the sisters' sun-hats.

"I'm sorry, Mrs Bad...Mrs Bradley—"

There was a titter from Esme. "I made them a daisy-chain each and I forgot about the hats."

"Forgot. You can't afford to forget with ladies of their age. Come along, girls. I think we've had enough of the sun."

She stared at Alan as she turned Esme's chair around. "I'm sure Albert has to go looking for his dog." Alan took the hint.

"I really do have to go," he said to Lily, who was struggling from her chair while leaning on her stick. Alan instinctively moved forward to help her.

"I'll do that!" Mrs Bradley snapped, leaving Esme's chair on the pathway.

"The Badger's in a bad mood today," Lily whispered as she winced in pain.

"I'll bring you some of the poems next time," Alan whispered in return.

As he turned to go, under Mrs Bradley's imperious stare, Esme waved to him even though her back was turned to him. "Goodbye, Albert. Do come again—soon—or I might be gone to Samarkand!"

"I will," Alan laughed. He didn't dare look at Mrs Bradley.

6

The Cemetery

ome on," Lisa called. "The grand tour of Kildavock and its outer suburbs is about to begin." She was standing astride her bike on the gravel outside Glebe House. Alan was ready to join her but his mother felt otherwise. "Your anorak. Have you got your anorak?"

"Mum, it's a warm summer day!"

"Yes, but you could have showers. Just pack this light anorak."

"Oh, Mum!"

After further cross-examination as to whether he had enough food and drink for the picnic, he escaped.

"Bye," Lisa and Alan called out as they cycled down the drive.

"Bye—and be careful. You're not used to

narrow country roads."

"Oh, Mum!" Alan muttered through gritted teeth.

"Mothers!" Lisa sighed. "What would we do without them?"

"Lots," Alan replied absentmindedly, "Lots."

"Come on, dreamer! Which of the many sights of Kildavock do you wish to see first?"

"Do you know where Mr Patterson lives?"

"Now there's a sight for you. He's real dishy! Sadly, he is bethroat—betrothed—and I must pine for him in my rustic cottage. I shall inevitably die of love, unloved!" She tossed her head and threw out an arm in a wildly dramatic gesture—a gesture which was totally ruined by her bicycle hitting a pothole. "Whoops!" she cried, as she wobbled all over the avenue, trying to regain control of the bike. Alan laughed helplessly and narrowly missed the same pothole himself.

"Really, Mr McKay! I would suggest you speak to your gardener about the state of your avenue." Lisa regained her haughty role. "My carriage was nearly ruined by his inattendance to his duties!" She paused and waited for Alan to draw level with her.

"In other words," she said, switching voices with ease, "me front wheel was nearly banjaxed!"

"You're a scream! You never told me you were

an actress!"

"I played a leading role in *The Wooing of Miss Wimpole*." She assumed the affected air of a film star. "It was said that there were at least two Hollywood scouts in the audience. I await a phone-call!" She couldn't maintain the pose any longer and exploded in infectious laughter. "Actually it was a performance by St Patrick's Youth Club in the parish hall, and we had audiences of twenty-five, twenty-two and—wait for it—fifty-one on the closing night! Were you ever in a play, Alan?"

"No."

They had turned onto the road and laboured up a hill. The road was completely arched over by tall beech trees on either side, affording them welcome shade from the noonday heat.

"Anyway,"—Lisa's voice was serious again—"Anyway, Mr Patterson's house is about two miles away—and he *is* dishy!" she added with a mischievous giggle. They freewheeled downhill and savoured the slight breeze in their faces. Lisa waved cheerily at the occupants of a car that passed them in the opposite direction.

"Do you know them?" Alan enquired.

"No."

"Then why do you—"

"Do it all the time. Just wave at them. You're

in the country now, Alan! Anyway, I love
watching their faces—trying to figure out 'who's
yer one?'"

Alan smiled, envious of her brazenness.

"Try it yourself," she called back to him,
reading his mind. He made a tentative wave at
the next car and grew bolder as they went on.
Soon they were both waving and calling wildly
at unsuspecting passers-by. An old man struggled
towards them on what seemed an even older
bike.

"How are ye?" he called. "Grand day!"

"Grand. Grand!" they replied in unison.

They were on level ground again. Lisa put on
her travel guide's voice. "We are now passing
one of Kildavock's main attractions, the local
football field. The scene of a mighty contest
tomorrow when Kildavock Emmets once again
meet Ballinabrack, the 'Barm Bracks', in the
championship and no doubt will once again be
walloped!"

"Sounds interesting!" Alan opined.

"Oh, you've got to be there and show the flag.
Tomorrow at three—and stay clear of Grandad.
He's a very different man at a football match!"

They cycled on and turned right just before
the village, down a winding road between patch-
work fields where cows lay lazily watching them

and constantly flicking their tails.

They came to a bungalow built on a slight rise at a bend on the road. Lisa stopped and gestured dramatically. "In yonder mansion lives the Reverend Mr Patterson. I feel I may swoon! Cease fluttering, O heart! 'Tis but the heat of the day!"

"Oh, come on, Lisa," Alan laughed. "There are no Hollywood scouts watching! I need to see this man!"

They left their bikes at the gate. It was shut tight as a safety precaution. On the neatly clipped lawn a little girl of about three was engaged in animated conversation with a doll in a pram. She completely ignored them.

Jane Patterson greeted them at the open front door. "It's our young historian," she said, smiling at Alan. He introduced Lisa. "You've come to see Stephen, I suppose?"

"Yes, please?" Lisa said cheekily.

Alan nudged her with his elbow as Jane turned away.

"He's in the study working on his sermon!"

Lisa winked at Alan. He jokingly shook his fist at her.

Stephen Patterson rose to greet them from his desk. He was tall and very dark. He combed back a shock of jet-black hair from his forehead with his fingers. "I'm glad of the interruption," he joked. "Working on a sermon is not the ideal way of spending a warm summer afternoon. I'd much prefer to be like Julie out there," he added, casting an envious eye on his daughter on the lawn. "Anyway, Jane tells me you're interested in the history of Glebe House."

As if on cue Jane arrived in with fizzy drinks and chocolate biscuits. "I told Alan you would have records of the rectors of the parish."

"Well, it depends on how far back you want to go."

"I'm only interested in one family—one rector —Mr Dixon—about seventy years ago," Alan stammered out, tentatively.

"Hmmm!" Mr Patterson knelt in front of the bookshelves that ran the length of one room. He fingered a number of slim volumes before withdrawing one of them. "1920. Hmmm! That's interesting—Cecil Dixon, Rector of Kildavock and Rathwarren 1900 to 1922—must be a record. I wonder if we'll be here for twenty-two years, Jane!"

"Does it mention any children?" Alan enquired before Jane could respond.

"No. It doesn't normally give family details. Why are you so interested in the Dixons, Alan?"

Alan was silent for a moment. He liked the

Pattersons. He felt they would understand. He decided to take them into his confidence. He took a deep breath and told the whole story of Lily and Esme.

"That's an amazing story!" Stephen Patterson was truly impressed. "To tell you the truth, I hadn't known of the Thompson sisters. I must pay them a visit."

"Did you ever hear of a...a ghost in Glebe House?" Alan asked, adding what Tom Grehan had told him.

"Can't say I have. It's probably a local yarn—"

"Knowing my grandad, it is very much a yarn!" Lisa laughed.

"What about Mr Grimshaw?" Jane interrupted.

"Mr Grimshaw?"

"Yes. He was the last rector to live in Glebe House. Lives in Dublin now, with his daughter. He must be quite old but he would know about the ghost—if there is a ghost."

"Do you know whereabouts in Dublin?" her husband asked.

"No. But I could make enquiries. Gosh! This is real Secret Seven stuff!"

"Except there are only four of us," Lisa added with a laugh. Then changing her tone, she asked, "Where would the Dixon family be buried?"

"Of course!" Stephen Patterson stood up suddenly. "Why didn't I think of that! The old cemetery at Rathwarren. Do you know it?"

"It happens to be the next stop on our grand tour of Kildavock."

They all stood up together.

"Thank you very much for your help," Alan said, as they edged towards the door.

"'Twasn't much, I'm afraid. Good luck with your adventure."

"With *our* adventure!" Jane corrected her husband. "I've got to get on the trail of Mr Grimshaw!"

It was only as they mounted their bikes to resume their journey that Julie Patterson noticed them and gave them a cheery wave.

"How far is Rathwarren?" Alan asked as they climbed another hill.

"Not far. A couple of miles. I fear I may not reach it. I feel faint!"

"Do you want to stop and rest?" Alan was suddenly concerned.

"No. 'Tis but a fluttering of my heart and the pain of parting from my loved one!" Lisa sighed in the most affected way possible.

"Oh, not again! You had me really worried there. You're the limit, Lisa, you really are!"

They were freewheeling downhill again.

"Mmm! That breeze is nice," Alan said, throwing his head back as they sped into a valley.

"It doth much to cool my fevered brow!" Lisa croaked weakly.

"Aaargh!" Alan cried in desperation and shot ahead of her.

The cemetery was small. A tall hedge concealed it from them initially. Only a rusting pair of ornate gates indicated something out of the usual beyond. It lay a field away, bounded by a low wall. Lisa and Alan wheeled their bikes across the field, along what was once a stony path but which was now largely overgrown with grass.

"We can have our picnic here," Alan said, "after we have found the grave."

"Brilliant place for a picnic!"

"Well, we won't be disturbed anyway."

"How do you know? I can see it now: a skeleton hand sneaking out from a vault and grabbing my ham and tomato sandwich..."

"Lisa! Your imagination's running away with you again!"

"Well, I can tell you if there's the slightest unusual move or sound I'll be out of there like a scalded cat—and my imagination won't be able to keep up with me!"

Alan laughed heartily. He enjoyed Lisa's humour, her openness. He enjoyed her company. He wondered if he would have got this far without her.

They parked their bikes at the boundary wall, took the picnic food from the carriers and climbed through a gap where the wall had come asunder. It was a crazy little place, full of mounds and hillocks, and very overgrown. Tombstones were tilted askew in all directions and there seemed to be no order or pattern to the place.

"The valley of the living dead! This is going to be great fun, I don't think," Lisa sighed, dropping her picnic bag.

"Look!" Alan cried. "There's a little ruin in the far corner. Must have been a church long ago." He pointed towards the remaining four walls of a small building no more than twenty feet long, nestling in a hollow on the other side of the cemetery. A tree had grown in the middle of the ruin.

"Legend has it that that is the ruin of the ninth-century St Davoc's Cell," Lisa intoned in her tourist guide voice, "and it is said that if maidens came here and walked three times around the cell chanting the name of the man they wished to marry, their wish would be granted within a year." She began to stride towards the ruin. "So I am going to chant—"

"You are going to help me search for the Dixon grave!" Alan commanded, grabbing her wrist as she brushed past him.

"Yes, master," she said meekly. "But I'm going to do it afterwards."

"We'll start here and work our way towards the ruin."

It was a difficult task, made more difficult by the sultry heat of the afternoon. Some tombstones were broken and lay upside down in the grass. Others were too old to be decipherable.

"Give me a hand to turn this one, Lisa," Alan asked.

Together they struggled with a particularly heavy stone. They tugged and heaved until at last the stone turned. Both of them collapsed on top of it.

"Brilliant!" Lisa snapped.

> *Sacred to the memory of*
> *Thomas Kingston*
> *Rathwarren House*
> *Called home*
> *15th Jan. 1852*

She chanted the details in a cynical voice as she traced them on the stone with her finger.

"He's well home by now—that's if he heard the call! Really, Alan, I think…"

Alan was no longer beside her. He was on his knees a few feet away, almost enfolding another headstone with his arms. "Look!" His voice dropped to a whisper. "Look, Lisa."

"Is it the Dixons?"

"No. It's…it's Lily and Esme's mother." They both read in silence.

> *Cecily Jane Thompson*
> *Beloved mother and wife*
> *Died 7th August 1917*
> *Aged 33 years*
> *Pray also for her husband*
> *David Reginald Thompson*
> *Lt Col Royal Inniskilling Fusiliers*
> *Killed in action 31st July 1917*
> *Aged 37 years*
> *Buried in Ypres, Belgium*
>
> *"We shall not forget them"*

Alan swallowed hard and strained his eyes open to stifle the tears that welled up.

"Oh, Alan, within a week. The two of them—orphaned!"

Alan couldn't speak. He stared at the

headstone. It disintegrated into jigsaw pieces which floated around before him. He chased them desperately, trying to hold them still but now the pieces floated in water which he realised was tears. He didn't know what to do. His first instinct was to run for his bike and get back to Lily and Esme. He would run across the meadow shouting, "I know! It's all right! I know!" but he realised there was little point in that.

"It's...all right to cry," Lisa suggested, rubbing her own eyes. "I think...I think we should take a rest and have the picnic now." It sounded stupid when she said it, but Alan nodded in agreement.

"You sit there. I'll get the stuff."

They ate in silence and took long drinks to slake their enormous thirst. "Can I go with you next time?" Lisa broke the silence.

"Where?"

"Down the chute—to see them. I'd like to meet them."

"I suppose so. How will I explain?"

"Just say I'm a friend—on holidays. They won't know—"

"How do you know—how do we know—what they know?" Alan snapped. "I'm sorry," he added immediately. "I'm not—I can't think very straight. Of course you can come."

He took his eyes off the headstone at last and looked around. They were in the middle of the cemetery. The ruin was only ten yards away. His sight was still blurred by tears. At first he thought it was a trick—his imagination playing on his confused state. He rubbed his eyes and looked again. It was no trick. He bounced up and started running towards the wall of the ruin.

"Alan! What is it now?" the startled Lisa cried as she stood up to follow him.

He was already at the ruin. A headstone backed onto the wall. It was more ornate than the others which ranged along the wall on either side of it. The figure of an angel was carved at the top of the stone. Underneath, in large faded lettering, one word was visible above the tall grass that covered the grave:

Dixon

Alan threw himself on the grass, flailing it with his arms in an effort to flatten it. The rest of the stone came into view:

Treasured memories of
Our darling only child
Albert Edward Dixon
Died tragically 5th August 1917

"Safe in the Arms of Jesus"

and also his mother
Emily Victoria Dixon
Died 19th November 1940
And his father
Cecil Walter Dixon
Rector of Kildavock and Rathwarren
Died 11th December 1941

Alan lay on the flattened grass and sobbed. Lisa knelt beside him and gently pinched the back of his neck.

"Oh, Alan!" she couldn't hold back the tears any longer.

"Don't you see?" His voice choked as he rose to a kneeling position.

"See?"

"The date! Look at the date! He—he died on their tenth birthday!"

Lisa instinctively threw her arms around Alan and hugged him.

They cycled home slowly. There was little conversation. Lisa tried to resume normality by pointing out other sights of Kildavock, but she knew it was futile. It took them a long time to reach the gates of Glebe House. Every hill seemed longer and steeper on the return journey.

"I'll go on to Granny's. Will you be all right?"

"Yes. I'm OK."

"I know it sounds stupid but—will you be at the match tomorrow?"

"The match?"

"Yeh. Emmets against—"

"The Barm Bracks. I remember!"

"It will take your mind off things—for a while."

"Yes. I'll be there. What time?"

"Half-past two. See you then?"

"Yeh. See you. And, Lisa—"

"What?"

"Thanks...thanks very much...for everything."

She was already moving off on her bike. "Think nothing of it!" She tossed her head haughtily. "Twas but a trifle. I must away to my rustic cottage!"

Her dramatic gestures caused her to wobble all over the road. Alan was smiling again as he turned into the avenue of Glebe House.

7

The Match

o *Sunday Times*! Third Sunday running." His father slammed the car door and drummed furiously on the steering wheel. "That's what you get for living in the sticks!" He glared at his wife. "Forty miles from Dublin and we might as well be in the Sahara Desert!"

"Michael, there's no need to go on like that. It's only a news—"

His answer was to start the car and rev the engine until it almost drowned her voice. "I'm going to Newbridge," he barked.

"Dad, can you drop me off at home first?" Alan asked.

"Why?"

"I'm going to the match."

"The match?"

"Yes. Football. Kildavock Emmets are playing Ball—"

"A football match! That's rich! Where did you get this sudden interest in football? You were never at a match in your life."

"Maybe it's because he was never brought," Alan's mother interrupted.

"Never brought? Who got him a ticket for a rugby international two years ago? And who wouldn't let him go just because of a few drops of rain?"

"I don't need to be brought. I'm going with Lisa." Alan didn't want another endless squabble.

"Why don't you bring the two of them?" his mother said coldly. "You might even enjoy it."

"Enjoy *that*? Bogmen killing each other. No thank you. Sunday is for relaxing—with the *Sunday Times*!"

The car roared off. Within minutes it screeched to a halt at the gates of Glebe House. His father reached into his pocket and pulled out a few pound coins. "Here," he said, giving them to Alan. "Get yourselves ice-cream or something." His voice had mellowed.

"Thanks," Alan said quietly. "You would enjoy it, Dad."

There was no reply. The engine was still running.

"I'll walk back with Alan," his mother said coldly. "Dinner will be at five."

They walked in silence for some time. Tatters broke the silence as he came excitedly to meet them.

"Your father's under a lot of pressure at work," his mother said eventually. Alan remained silent. "Don't ask me the reason. I could never understand high finance. But since he was put in charge of the Financial Services Division, he really has had to work hard. I'm trying to get him to take a break."

Alan threw a stick for Tatters to fetch. There was nothing he could say.

"Now what's this about a football match?" His mother's voice acquired an anxious tone.

"It's just a match—in the local field."

"Will you be safe...on your own?"

"Oh, Mum. There won't be riots or anything! And anyway I won't be on my own. Lisa and her grandad will be there."

"You like Lisa, don't you?"

"She's good fun."

"Well, take care. You never know what could happen at these games."

"Oh, Mum!"

Lisa was waiting on the road outside the football field. Alan was quite surprised at the line of cars that was parked along the roadside. People were moving in twos and threes towards the gate where a man was collecting money.

"Thought you weren't coming," Lisa said.

"I had to go back home with Tatters; he kept following me."

"You could have brought him as a mascot. He wears the same colours as the Emmets!"

Just then there was a rousing cheer as the local team ran onto the field, dressed in a black-and-white strip.

"You never told me," Alan laughed. "I'll bring him next time!"

"Next year that will be. The Emmets always get beaten by this lot!"

"This lot" appeared on the field to a lesser cheer from the far side of the field. Cries of "Come on the Bracks" accompanied the waving of green-and-red flags, as the teams lined up for the throw-in. Alan and Lisa found a good vantage point on the sloping bank.

"There's Grandad," said Lisa, pointing to a knot of men standing at the foot of the bank. "If the match gets boring, watch him instead!"

The match was anything but boring. Both sides tore into the action with great gusto and the crowd's excitement grew steadily. Alan was soon caught up in the excitement as all around

him the supporters' cries echoed the ebb and
flow of the game.

"Get stuck into them, Emmets."

"Bracks' ball—ah, ref!"

"Stay with him, Reilly. Stay with him."

"Couldn't kick snow off a rope!"

"Great ball!"

Alan joined in the shouting, giving encouragement to the home team, criticising the
referee's decisions and making fun of the Barm
Bracks' every move. Half-time came too soon for
him although it did give himself and Lisa a
chance to buy choc-ices and move down to Tom
Grehan for his reaction to the game. Tom greeted
him with a wink. "I think we'll do it. Only a
point behind. If the forwards only take half their
chances, we're home and dry."

They moved back to their place for the second
half. The play was as furious as ever and Alan
felt his throat ache with a terrible dryness as he
urged on Kildavock. The Emmets gradually took
control and went two points in front as the game
neared its end. Then, disaster! A Ballinabrack
forward was brought down as he tried to work
his way into the Kildavock goal-mouth. Penalty!
After the initial howls of protest, a strange silence
descended on the Kildavock supporters. Alan
couldn't bear to look but the sudden eruption of

cheers from the far side of the field told him the
worst had happened. The last few minutes of
the match were a blur. Screams of desperation
from the Emmets' supporters were to no avail.
Alan found himself screaming too, praying that
somehow Kildavock would manage just one point
to draw level with Ballinabrack. In between
screams his voice dropped to a hoarse whisper.
"Please! Please let them! Please! Just one!
Please!"

And then a long burst on the referee's whistle.
An eerie silence descended on the Kildavock
side of the field. In the distance there was wild
cheering, but all around Alan people just looked
at each other in disbelief. Lisa wiped a tear from
her eye and shrugged her shoulders. "Let's go,"
she whispered. "I don't want to get caught up in
Grandad's post-mortems!"

Alan looked down at the familiar stooped
shoulders of Tom Grehan who stood with a small
group of men who were busy lighting cigarettes
and arguing among themselves as to where the
game was won and lost. Tom was pointing to
one corner of the pitch and at the same time
gesturing wildly to the other end of the field
with his left arm. He then threw both arms in
the air and tossed his head back. "The post-
mortem will obviously go on for a while," Alan

laughed weakly.

"For a few hours in Byrne's pub," Lisa sighed as she pulled her bike out of the hedge.

They cycled slowly up the road, weaving their way through small groups who walked disconsolately along the middle of the road, paying no heed to the cars which edged their way from the grass verge. When they had got clear of the pedestrians a car shot past them up the hill. A head appeared out of a rear window. "Yehoooo! Come on the Bracks!" They both shook their fists at the speeding car.

"Ye were steeped in luck!" Lisa called after them.

They cycled on in silence until Lisa stopped at a rusting gateway. "Have you thought any more about—them?" she asked, nodding her head over the gate.

"Them?"

"Lily and Esme. That's their house away over there."

"But it can't—of course. We're looking at it from a different direction. I've never actually seen the front of the house."

"Well, have you?" There was no reply. "Alan, come in. Are you receiving me?"

"Oh sorry! Have I...?"

Lisa growled in frustration. She put on a

computer voice, holding her nose. "*Have you thought about Lily and Esme? Do they speak English on your planet? Over.*"

Alan laughed in embarrassment. "Always knew you were an alien! Of course I've thought about them—a lot. I'm just confused. About their parents. And their birthday. We'll have to do something for their birthday. And—" He fell silent.

"And?"

"You'll probably think this is…stupid."

"Try me."

"It's Albert. Albert Dixon. Dying on their birthday. It gives me a weird feeling."

Lisa adopted a Count Dracula voice. "Like you think it might be your turn this time!"

"I knew you'd think it was stupid."

"I didn't say it was stupid. I often put on these voices when I'm…nervous of something."

There was silence. Lisa mounted her bike again. Alan followed.

"So when are you going to see them?"

"Tomorrow, I hope. Can you come?"

"No—and you can't either!"

"What do you mean?"

"Tomorrow is for the bog. We're going turf-cutting, and Grandad needs someone—correction—some *two* to spread the turf!"

"Spread it?"

"You'll find out all about the joys of spreading turf tomorrow!"

They had reached the gate of Glebe House. "We'll pick you up in the 'limo' at nine, OK?— that is if Grandpapa survives today's most awful disappointment and the dreadful goings-on which are at this moment taking place at ye olde tavern in the village. I fear I may have to send the butler in a carriage to fetch him home!"

"Please," Alan giggled. "No more!"

"All right. But I shall remember that when I am a famous actress! Byeee!"

She freewheeled down the hill with legs outstretched.

"And Alan!" she called without looking back.

"Yes?" he shouted.

"I don't think it was stupid. Byeee!"

His father was sitting on a deck-chair under a parasol on the lawn in front of the house. He put an iced drink under the chair as he wrestled with various sections of the *Sunday Times*.

"At least he'll be happier now," Alan thought as he rode up.

"Well, it's the football fan," his father announced, peering over his sun-glasses. "Did ye win?"

"No. Beaten by a point."

"A point! Were there riots? Pitch invasions?"

"No. Just a lot of sad faces."

"Listen, son." His father moved uncomfortably as he reached for his drink. "The things I said earlier—about you going to the match and— saying they were bogmen—that stuff. Just forget I said it."

"It's OK."

"I was just uptight about not getting the paper." He tried once more to open and fold a particular section. "And now that I have it, it's a major struggle to get through it. I'm convinced the only contented reader of the *Sunday Times* is an octopus!"

Alan laughed openly. It was seldom he found his father in such humour. "Dad, Tom Grehan wants me to help him on the bog tomorrow. Is that—"

His father peered at him once again and then exploded into laughter. Alan stood open-mouthed before him.

"That's priceless!" his father spluttered as he struggled out of the chair and went towards the house. "Deirdre, did you hear that? I just apologised to Alan about the 'bogmen' bit—and now he wants..." His voice trailed away as he went through the house. It was only then that the humour of the situation dawned on Alan.

8

The Bog

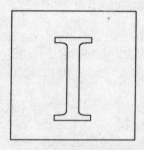t took repeated reassur-
ances from Tom Grehan
next morning before his
mother finally released Alan for a day on the
bog. "And keep well away from the bogholes,"
she called as the van moved down the avenue.
Alan squirmed with embarrassment in the back
of the van as Lisa, sitting opposite, wagged a
threatening finger in time with his mother's
words. "This is Heels Dunne," Tom broke the
awkward silence. "Best man in Kildavock with
a *sleán!*"

"That's the yoke you're sitting on," Lisa
answered the question that was in his mind.
"It's for cutting turf." He ran his hand along
the smooth handle that lay under him. The
handle tapered into what looked like a two-
headed spade. "Good man yourself!" Heels Dunne

half-turned in the passenger seat and offered his hand in greeting. He was a small squat figure, occupying the entire space between Tom and the passenger door. "Hi!" Alan said as his hand was smothered in the huge grip of Heels's gnarled hand.

"Well," said Tom as the van laboured up a steep incline, "what did you think of the match?"

"Ye—we were unlucky!" His comment galvanised Heels.

"Unlucky is right! Unlucky we had that big latchico Reilly at full-forward. I tell you if I had anything to do with that team I wouldn't even let that big stook of straw carry the water-bottle. That fellow wouldn't hit a haybarn from the inside!"

"Ah, he wasn't the only one, Heels!"

"They're off!" Lisa laughed, rolling her eyes upward.

The argument continued between the two men as the van rattled along a stony by-road for some miles before turning down what was little more than a gravel track. They had climbed to a high plateau. Before them the track wound glinting in the sunlight like a snail's path through the green, purple and black of what seemed an endless bogland. The van stopped suddenly. Tom beeped the horn and put his head out the window.

"I'll send them down for the tea about one, Lena. Make it good and strong!" He waved and moved off again. Alan squinted through the back window to see a plump dark-haired woman, dressed in a fold-over apron, waving from the door of a tiny tin-roofed cottage.

"That's Lena Ryan," Lisa called. "Lives there on her own. Her mother died last year but Lena won't move."

The track grew more uneven. Alan and Lisa bobbed up and down on the bare floor of the van and sighed together with relief when the journey finally ended. It was a joy to stand up straight and stretch cramped arms and legs. Alan stared spellbound at the vast wilderness that stretched before him. The day was already quite warm and the strong sunlight picked out the many shades of colour in the heather and gorse. In the distance a few figures moved about where a patch of black stood out in the heather. Work had already begun for some.

"Come on, Master McKay. There's work to be done!" Tom handed him a hold-all. "That's the food. You're in charge of the kitchen!" They set off across the bog. The men, implements held aloft on their shoulders, picked their way along a well-beaten track. Alan decided he would be more adventurous and began hopping from one mound to another. He had only taken three hops when he sank to his ankles in a black ooze. "Old Chinese proverb," Lisa jibed. "In the bog nothing is what it seems!" Tom paused to pull a barrow from where it had been concealed in a dried-up ditch. He wheeled it a short distance to the edge of a bog-hole. It was an unusual barrow, made of wooden slats with just a floor and one side tilting over the wheel. The men prepared for work, rolling up sleeves and tucking trouser-ends into socks.

"Here," Lisa called, throwing him a battered sun-hat.

"I'm not wearing *that*!" Alan spluttered.

"Yes you are and you'll be glad of it, unless you want the neck and shoulders burned off you," Lisa retorted firmly as she adjusted an even more battered hat on herself. Alan noticed that Heels Dunne and Tom Grehan had improvised their own headgear. Heels had produced a huge peaked cap and propped it on his head back to front so that the peak shaded his neck. Tom had knotted a large white handkerchief at each corner and was pulling it firmly down on his balding head. What a comical lot we are, Alan thought as he reluctantly pulled on the sun-hat.

"Right," Tom called. "We'll make a start. Lisa

will show you what to do, Alan. Heels is ready to play the game of his life down there!"

Heels stood on a glistening platform of wet peat on a level about five feet below the edge where the others stood. He spat on his hands, muttered "In the name of God," sliced the *sleán* into the peat and deftly tossed a long wet sod up to Tom who caught it and placed it on the barrow. "'Tis an awful pity we haven't Toss Reilly here to do the catching, Heels!" said Tom with an impish wink to Alan and Lisa. There was a muttered obscenity from below and the sods came flying up at a furious rate. "'Tis the only way to get him going. Annoy him!" Tom whispered as he piled the sods on the barrow. When it was full he wheeled it away from the turf-bank and emptied it on the heather some distance away. "Now, off ye go!"

Alan watched as Lisa lifted the sods from the pile and spread them out to dry under the sun. "Simple!" she said. "That's all you have to do!" Simple it looked but Alan was amazed at how heavy the sleek dripping sods were. He lifted the sod gingerly at first, holding it away from his tee-shirt. "Ah, come on, Alan," Lisa laughed, squelching the sod up against his chest, "Mammy isn't watching you now!" He relished the cool wetness of the sod and sank his fingers into it only to find it broke in two in his hands. "Clumsy!" Lisa taunted him. He was about to daub her face with his black wet hand when Tom arrived with another barrowload. From then on it was back-breaking work, bending, lifting, turning the glistening sods. Alan had never known work so hard. They spread each barrowload as quickly as they could so that they could flop backwards on the heather and rest before Tom appeared with another barrowload. As if his aching back and legs were not enough, the hunger pangs soon added to Alan's discomfort. The sun climbed higher and burned his arms and legs. "Told you you'd be glad of the hat," Lisa sang. "And you look gorgeous in it!" He chased after her, stumbling blindly through the heather.

"Come on, kitchen department!" Tom called. "Time to eat!" His words were music to their ears.

"Freedom from the slave camp! Race you to Lena's!" Lisa called. They practically fell into Lena's doorway.

"My, but ye're the lively pair!" Lena laughed. "And who's this fine big man?"

"We're not alive, Lena. We're the walking dead," Lisa sighed, flopping into a súgán chair. "And this zombie is called Alan."

The room was cool and dark, a welcome refuge from the noonday heat. "Let ye take your ease while the kettle is boiling," Lena said, offering them a glass of diluted orange drink each. Alan savoured every drop that slipped down his parched throat. The kettle soon began to sing on the open hearth. Alan was intrigued by the novelty of the fire with its various crooks suspended from the dark chimney. Lena hummed to herself as she busily filled two cans of tea from the huge black kettle. Nobody spoke. It was just what Alan and Lisa wanted: a cool, peaceful and welcoming place.

"Off ye go now," said Lena, securing the lids on the cans. "The hotter the tea is on a day like this the better. And here's a little extra. Soda bread hot off the griddle! 'Tis buttered and all. Your grandad loves that, Lisa. Goodbye now. God bless ye."

Alan didn't want to leave.

"Come on, zombie!" Lisa called.

"Thank you," Alan said. "We'll call again."

"Do indeed. A soul gets lonely out here at times."

They hurried back as quickly as the full cans would allow them. Alan opened up the hold-all. Mrs Grehan had gauged their hunger well. The bag was teeming with an assortment of sandwiches: tomato, egg, ham, and his own favourite, cucumber. The four ate in silence. Never did food taste so good. Alan wolfed the sandwiches and savoured the tea.

"God bless Lena," Tom said at last. "No-one can make tea like her."

"'Tis the spring water," Heels mumbled through a sandwich.

"And she has a surprise for you," Lisa added, unwrapping the soda bread. Tom's face lit up like a child's at Christmas time. "Lord save us, Heels. We'll do no more work after this." The soda bread was still warm and generously soaked in butter. It was delicious.

"I'll bet you never ate at home like this, young fella," Heels chuckled. He was right.

"Heels," Alan asked, at ease in the company, "why do they call you Heels?"

"Because he always showed a clean pair of heels to the law when he was in trouble," Tom giggled.

"That's not true, Grandad," Lisa interrupted. "It's the steel in the heels of your boots, isn't it, Heels?"

"That's right, young lassie. Ever since Father Gannon made a crowd of us move from the porch up to the front seat of the church."

"Heehee!" Tom chuckled. "I remember it well.

You could hear the studs in his heels ringing off the floor of the church a mile away!"

"I never forgave him for that," Heels said as he cleaned his teeth with a straw.

Alan lay back on the heather and savoured the slight pine-scented breeze. He noticed a puff-ball of cloud overhead and thought of Samarkand, of Esme and Lily.

"Does anyone know of a poet called Ledwidge?" he asked dreamily. Silence. Then to Alan's amazement Heels cleared his throat and, looking into the distance, began to recite:

"He shall not hear the bittern cry
In the wild sky, where he is lain,
Nor voices of the sweeter birds
Above the wailing of the rain.

"Nor shall he know when loud March blows
Thro' slanting snows her fanfare shrill
Blowing to flame the golden cup
Of many an upset daffodil.

"And when the Dark Cow leaves the moor,
And pastures poor with greedy weeds,
Perhaps he'll hear her low at morn
Lifting her horn in pleasant meads.

"'The Lament for Thomas MacDonagh' by

Francis Ledwidge, the Poet of the Blackbird. Born 1887. Killed in action 1917."

There was a pause before Alan instinctively applauded the performance.

"Heels never learned much at school but he used to meet them coming home!" laughed Tom.

"Learned that from my father," Heels replied, still looking into the distance. "He was a great one for the verse, God be good to him. Now," he said, jumping up suddenly and changing his tone, "is there anyone for work around here?"

They worked for another few hours. At first Alan felt refreshed by the rest and the food but as the afternoon wore on, the aches returned to his limbs and his movements grew slower.

"That'll do us!" Tom said eventually, and Alan gratefully sat on the empty barrow.

"We'll have to wheel this man home, Lisa," he laughed, putting his hand on Alan's shoulder. "You won't forget your first day on the bog in a hurry! But we've done well!"

Alan surveyed the turf they had spread. They had done well.

"Here," Tom said, pressing something into Alan's hand. "You've earned that!"

It was a five-pound note. He felt a thrill running through his aching body, not at having earned five pounds but at being accepted and praised as one of a team.

They loaded up the van and Alan and Lisa tumbled into the back. The bumpy gravel-track didn't seem to bother them any more. Tom stopped at Lena's house to return the cans.

"That tea is worth a load of turf any day, Lena," Heels said.

"And the soda bread is worth another," Tom added.

"I'll be all right for firing for the winter so," Lena laughed. "God bless ye and safe home." She put her head in the window. "And don't forget to call into me again, you two!"

"We won't," Alan and Lisa replied together.

"My God, Alan—look at the state of your clothes!" were his mother's words of greeting.

"'Tis only clean dirt from the bog," Tom Grehan called from the van. "Go easy on him now! He did a great day's work." They drove off.

"The shower is the first place for you—and then bed. You look wrecked."

Alan didn't object. He showered, put on clean clothes and lay on his bed. His mother came into the room. "Well, that's an improvement! By the way, Mr Patterson—the rector—called and left these for you. Said he got them in the library. I won't even begin to ask why you need them but at least it's a change from what you usually read!" She handed him two books, *Francis Ledwidge: Complete Poems* and *Francis Ledwidge: a Life of the Poet*.

Alan smiled. "Thanks, Mum. It's just a kind of project I'm doing with Lisa." His mother withdrew from the room. He began to leaf through the *Complete Poems*, but before he could read even one of them, sleep had descended on him.

9

The Poet

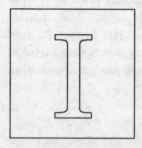t was ten o'clock the following morning before he awoke. A blanket had been draped over him during the night. The two books lay on the locker beside him. He picked up *Life of the Poet* and idly flicked through it. Details of Ledwidge's life filtered through to him. "Born into poverty in County Meath. Wrote poetry from an early age. In a row with rival football supporters who 'insulted his team'."

Alan smiled. Come on, Kildavock, he thought.

"World War. Joined the British Army. The Inniskilling Fusiliers…"

The Inniskilling Fusiliers—where have I seen that before? he thought. The cemetery—the grave—Lily and Esme's father. He flicked on through the pages.

"Gallipoli. Horrific battles. 19,000 of his comrades

killed. His first book, *Songs of the Fields*, published in 1916."

Alan paused. "Father sent it all the way from the front. Even got Mr Ledwidge to sign it for him. Father says Mr Ledwidge is going to be Ireland's greatest poet…" He turned the pages with growing curiosity. "Home again. Easter Rising 1916. Leaders executed, among them Thomas MacDonagh…'He shall not hear the bittern cry…'" Alan could see Heels Dunne looking across the bog.

"To war again. December 1916. France. Ypres. Ypres." How do you pronounce that? Where have I seen it? The grave…"31 July 1917. Ledwidge and his comrades road-making in torrential rain. A shell exploded beside them. Blown to bits. 31 July 1917."

The date. The same date. Their father and Ledwidge died together. Alan closed the book. Another part of the jigsaw was complete.

It was almost midday. He heard voices downstairs, then footsteps approaching. Lisa appeared in the doorway. "You lazy sod of turf! Still in bed and half the day gone."

"Not at all!" He remembered he was fully dressed and jumped out of bed. "I was simply taking a siesta—and don't even mention sods of turf!"

"I know! I know! Even my aches have aches! What are you reading?"

He told her about the books and what he had learned about Ledwidge. Lisa was more interested in the source of the books. "You mean that my loved one came and I was not here to receive him! Oh, my heart quickens at the thought!"

"Oh, give over, Lisa! Don't you see what this means? Ledwidge, their father, their mother all died within a few days of each other—"

"And Albert." .

"And Albert."

"Don't you wonder how he died?"

"All the time. All it said on the tombstone was 'tragically'. That could be anything: fire, drowning—anything."

There was a pause in the conversation. Alan laced up his runners.

"The attic room," Lisa spoke almost absent-mindedly. "It must have something to do with the attic room."

"Why?"

"Well, isn't that where the so-called ghost appears? Why does he appear at that window? Can't we get in there—to discover the secret of the attic room?" she added in a sinister voice.

"It's not funny, Lisa—and anyway it's all

boarded up. I tried."

"Oooh, but we are tetchy today!" Lisa picked up the *Complete Poems* of Francis Ledwidge.

"Sorry," he blurted. "It's just—"

"Are you going to see the girls today?"

"Yes. Do you want to come?"

"Why do you think I'm standing here, dumbo?"

When they climbed down the chute, Alan was surprised and disappointed to find that the meadow had been mowed since his last visit. "Badger will have no trouble seeing us now," he muttered. They had also failed to escape without Tatters, who now bounded about enjoying the freedom of the open field. The sisters were in their usual corner of the clearing. Esme in the wheelchair, Lily with the stick.

"Hello," Alan said nervously. "I've brought a friend."

"Did you find her in Australia?" Esme asked diffidently.

"No, in Kildavock," Alan replied weakly. "This is Lisa."

"Hello," Lisa chirped.

"Don't mind Esme, Lisa," Lily explained. "She's just in bad form because Badger was cross with her. Esme was a bold girl this morning!"

"What did you do, Esme?" Lisa enquired.

"Hmph. Just spilled some tea," Esme grumbled.

"Just spilled it on Badger's dress," Lily giggled. Alan and Lisa giggled with her. Esme remained silent.

"I see you brought that Ruffian fellow!" she muttered. "I hope he doesn't go chasing Tickles again."

"Oh, Esme, you really are a grumpy boots this morning," Lily reprimanded her sister.

"I—I brought the—book too," Alan said, knowing that it wasn't "the book" but hoping they wouldn't ask for it.

"Oh, good!" Esme brightened up. "Do read something for us, Albert."

"Yes, do," Lily echoed.

Alan fumbled at the book. He hadn't had time to look through it. Nor had he ever read much poetry—of any kind. He opened it at random.

"Here's one called 'June'." His hands were shaking. He read slowly, nervously, badly, but he kept going.

> *"Broom out the floor now, lay the fender by,*
> *And plant this bee-sucked bough*
> *of woodbine there,*
> *And let the window down. The butterfly*
> *Floats in upon the sunbeam..."*

Lisa sat on the grass, fondling Tatters. She watched the sisters as Alan read. Their faces glowed. Esme nodded gently to the rhythm of the words. Lily, head aloft, looked into the distance.

> *"And loop this red rose in that hazel ring*
> *That snares your little ear, for June is short*
> *And we must joy in it and dance and sing.*
> *And from her bounty draw her rosy worth.*
> *Ay! soon the swallows will be flying south,*
> *The wind wheel north to gather in the snow,*
> *Even the roses spilt on youth's red mouth*
> *Will soon blow down the road all roses go."*

"Lovely!" Esme cried, clapping her twisted and swollen hands.

"I love the roses part," Lily said. "Father calls us his two little roses, doesn't he, Esme? His roses of Picardy."

To the amazement of Alan and Lisa, Esme began to sing, haltingly, a snatch of a song

> *"Roses are shining in Picardy*
> *In the hush—"*

She faltered, then picked up the song again:

> *"Roses are flowering in Picardy*
> *But there's never a rose like you."*

She stopped.

"That's lovely, Esme," Lisa whispered.

"Picardy, that's where he is," Lily explained. "It's in France. He showed us—on the map— before he—left." Her voice trailed away.

"Read another one, Albert," Esme said softly. Alan thumbed through the pages again. "This one is called 'Home'—

> *"A burst of sudden wings at dawn,*
> *Faint voices in a dreamy noon,*
> *Evenings of mist and murmurings*
> *And nights with rainbows of the moon.*
>
> *"And through these things a wood-way dim*
> *And waters dim, and slow sheep seen*
> *On uphill paths that wind away*
> *Through summer sounds and harvest green.*
>
> *"This is a song a robin sang*
> *This morning on a broken tree;*
> *It was about the little fields*
> *That call across the world to me."*

" 'The little fields that call across the world to

me,'" Esme repeated. "I do hope Father brings Mr Ledwidge to see us. He promised he would."

Alan stole a glance at Lisa.

"I just wish Father would write to us," Lily sighed.

"It's probably difficult for post to get through," Alan suggested, not daring to look at anyone.

"That's what Badger keeps saying," Lily replied, "but—"

Their conversation was interrupted by Tatters tearing off in pursuit of a big ginger cat who made for the safety of the drooping ash tree.

"Tickles! Tickles!" Esme called. "I knew this would happen. Really, Albert, I wish you would leave that dog at home."

"I tried—" Alan blurted out.

"She won't come down for ages now. That's what happened the last time." Esme peered anxiously through the leafy branches.

"Don't worry," Alan reassured her. "I'll get her down. Lisa, you hold Tatters—Ruffian." He searched for a foothold and began climbing the stout trunk of the ash.

"Be careful, Albert," Lily called.

"I'm all right," he grunted as he reached the first large branch. Tickles greeted his arrival by moving further up the tree and along another branch five feet above him. "Drat!" Alan hissed.

"Here, pussy! Here, Tickles," he called.

Lily was growing more agitated. "Leave her, Albert. Come down. Remember—"

"It's just the next branch," he called back. He had reached the branch and began inching his way along. As he did so the branch began to wave up and down. Alan grew uneasy. The cat turned and faced him but refused to respond to his coaxing.

"Albert!" Lily had struggled with the help of her stick to the foot of the tree. "Albert! Please come down. Remember, you don't like heights!"

"Yes," Esme called from a distance. "We don't want you falling again!"

"I'm all right. I'm all right!" he could hear the tremor in his own voice. "I'm nearly there!" He felt the branch bend more as he moved along.

"Albert!" Lily was beginning to shake.

"Al—bert?" Lisa called. "I think you should leave it."

He was almost within reach of the cat when it turned and gave a flying leap to the branch below and from there to the ground.

"Thanks a lot, cat," he muttered and began to move backwards along the bough.

"What's going on here? Who is this girl?" He recognised the grating voice of Mrs Bradley.

"This is Lisa, a friend of Albert's," Esme

explained.

"Albert was up the tree trying to rescue Tickles, but Tickles got down by—"

"Oh, all right, Esme," Mrs Bradley snapped impatiently, as she helped Lily back to her chair.

"She was only explaining—" Lisa began.

"Did I ask you, child?" she glared at the girl.

"No, but I'm telling you anyway," Lisa retorted cheekily.

By this time Alan had slithered down the trunk of the tree. Mrs Bradley turned to him. "What do you mean, causing these ladies such worry and fright? Look at the state of them!"

"I was—"

"I don't want excuses! Can't you see you've upset them greatly?" She gestured towards the still trembling Lily.

"You say you're their friend. Yet every time you come there's trouble," she continued, spewing the words at him. "Now it's time for their rest. I suggest you take that infernal dog and your —" she paused, looking at Lisa from head to toe—"cheeky friend with you."

"Charmed, I'm sure," Lisa muttered. "Come, Albert. Our carriage awaits!"

"Goodbye, little roses!"

"Goodbye, Lisa," Esme called. There was no response from Lily. Albert went over to her.

"I didn't mean to upset you, Lily. Honest. I was only trying to help."

"I—didn't want you—to fall—again," Lily croaked.

"Come along, Lily!" Mrs Bradley began to help the old woman to her feet, glowering at Alan as she did so. He put his hand on Lily's slender, wrinkled fingers.

"Goodbye," he whispered. "I'll see you soon."

Alan chewed a blade of hay as they strolled back across the new-mown meadow.

"Well, what do you think?" he asked, throwing a quick glance over his shoulder at the figure in black helping Lily back to the house.

"I think there's a strong case for the extermination of badgers," Lisa replied through gritted teeth. "She's a monster."

Alan laughed nervously. "I meant about Lily and Esme."

"Oh. They're cute. They really have a thing about you."

"Not about me. About Albert."

"What's the difference—to them? It's weird though."

"What is?"

"When you're with them, it's easy to believe it's seventy years ago or whatever."

"I know."

"You don't sort of—have to pretend."

"I know."

They climbed the chute back into Alan's garden.

"Lily really did get upset about you, Alan. She was shaking life a leaf. That's why I called—"

"I know."

"Will you for God's sake stop saying 'I know' all the time!"

"Sorry. I was just thinking of why Lily was upset—and what she said."

"Which was?"

"She kept saying she was afraid I'd fall again."

"So?"

"So Albert must have had a fall."

"Oh?"

They reached the house.

"Jiminy! It's three o'clock. I'll be murdered!" Lisa jumped on her bike and sped down the avenue. "I'll see you!" she called. "And Alan."

"Yeh?"

"You're a lousy reader of poetry!"

"I know!" he shouted after her.

"Well, here comes the poet of Kildavock!" his father greeted him at dinner.

"I'm not a poet," Alan replied sheepishly.

"What's this I hear then about the rector

arriving with books of poetry?"

"It was only one book of poetry. It's just a project I'm doing with Lisa—for her school," he added, compounding the lie.

"Which reminds me," his mother interjected, "we have to talk about your school, Alan. Your father and I have been thinking—well, summer is flying past—and we have to think about secondary school."

"What your mother is trying to say," his father said briskly, "is that we've arranged for you to board at my old school. 'Twasn't easy to get you in at this late stage but I—"

"I'm not going," Alan blurted out.

"What do you mean you're not going?"

"I don't want to go away to boarding school. I don't like boarding school."

"But you haven't been to one, Alan. You won't know till—"

He interrupted his mother. "I don't like the idea. I can go to school in Newbridge."

"Now listen, young man," his father's voice had an impatient edge, "I went to considerable trouble to get you into this place. There's a waiting list of three years. It just happens that I get on well with the president, since my rugby-playing days. And stuff this nonsense about 'I don't like the idea.' They've got tremendous facilities—the best. You'll make friends—boy friends." There was more than a hint of sarcasm in the last comment.

"You can make boy friends in any school," Alan countered.

"It's not like the old boarding school, Alan," his mother pleaded. "You'll be home every second weekend."

"I'd rather come home every evening."

"Ah, for crying out loud!" His father shoved his coffee-cup away in disgust. "Home to what, for God's sake. To football matches and working in the bog."

"What's wrong with that?"

"That's enough cheek out of you, sir. What you need is some of the corners knocked off you and boarding school is the place to do that. You go there in September. End of story!" He stormed out of the room.

"He has a point, you know," his mother said softly.

"So have I, Mum." He surprised himself by saying that. His mother busied herself clearing the table. Alan went outside and walked down the avenue, occasionally throwing a stick for Tatters to fetch. If his father knew that one of the reasons he didn't want to go away was his friendship with two old ladies he would throw a fit altogether! But that wasn't the only reason. He just didn't like the idea of boarding school. And he did like men like Tom Grehan and Heels Dunne. There wasn't much in Kildavock but what there was he liked. It wasn't the end of the story. It wasn't.

He had reached the gate. He sat on the grassy bank at the roadside. Tatters sat in anticipation of further chases. A car approached, slowed down and stopped just opposite him.

"A penny for your thoughts!" It was Jane Patterson's cheery voice. "I've got good news for you! I've located Mr Grimshaw. You know—the old rector. So you and I and Lisa have a secret appointment in Dublin on Saturday afternoon! Is that OK?"

"It's great! Thanks. Thanks very much."

"And don't worry! As far as your Mum and Dad are concerned, we're just going to do some shopping. The Secret Four forever! See you Saturday at two. Byee!"

The car moved off before he could reply. He waved to her and saw her return the wave before the car disappeared over the brow of the hill. No. It wasn't the end of the story.

"Come on, Tatters! Race you back to the house."

10

The Letter

t wouldn't work. They're not *that* dotty!"

"Of course it would," Lisa argued, "if you left it to me. You are dealing with a superior brain here. One of the great undiscovered writers of our time."

"Like the great undiscovered actress!"

"You may sneer! My time has yet to come! And as to my writing talent may I remind you that I won third prize in the 'Wexford in the 1990s' essay competition."

"How many entries were there?"

"Eight—but that is not the point! The judges said I was 'very creative'."

They were sitting on the front steps of Glebe House. A lowering sky threatened an afternoon of rain. Lisa slapped her face. "I hate those midgets! A sure sign of rain."

"Midges!"

"I beg your pardon?"

"Midges. They're called midges, not midgets.
Midgets are—"

"Midgets is what we call them in Wexford—
a county noted for its culture—" she added in a
haughty voice, "and its undiscovered writers!"

A roll of thunder signalled the first drops of
rain which splattered on the steps. They
scampered inside.

"Look," Lisa said as she tucked her legs under
her body in an armchair in the television room,
"what is the one thing that Lily and Esme go on
about most?"

"Their father being away in France."

"Correct. And what would cheer them up more
than anything else in the whole wide world?"

"A letter from their father."

"Two out of two. There's hope for us yet!"

"So what's wrong with us making up that
letter?"

"It's cheating."

"Cheating? *Cheating*? Who's cheating—pre-
tending to be a boy from seventy years ago?"

"That's different! They saw me—see me—as
Albert."

"Exactly. So what's wrong with creating
another part of that world and doing something

that will make them happy?"

"Nothing, I suppose. But what about the postman—and Badger opening the letter?"

"Not a problem. Jimmy Dempsey is the laziest postman in the country. We just tell them we met Jimmy on the road and he gave us the letter to deliver."

"But the handwriting—and the stamp and—"

"God, is it the weather that has dampened your brain? The roses aren't up to examining stamps or even reading a letter. You'll offer to read it for them."

"I still don't know what we'll put in it—to make it convincing."

"Your mother should have called you Thomas —Doubting Thomas! Didn't you tell me that Ledwidge's letters are in that book? We can draw on those. We have enough details to compose a good letter—if you just leave the composing to me. Now fetch me a writing-pad, boy and that book!"

"It's crazy—but it might just work!"

"Conversion—at last!"

For the next hour, Lisa was deep in concentration, flicking through the Ledwidge biography, chewing the top of her pen and then launching into sustained writing bursts. She would not tolerate any interruptions. Alan began to look idly through Ledwidge's *Complete Poems*. He paused.

"Lisa?"

"Shhh. Busy!"

"Can I make a suggestion?"

"Mmmm?"

"Just one suggestion?"

"If you really must interrupt my creative flow—"

"I've come across a poem here which might be of use to you, that's all."

She read the poem.

"Brilliant! Thank you!" She resumed writing at a furious pace. Ten minutes later she was finished. She handed the pages to Alan and went to watch the rain while he read.

"Well?"

"It's—great! I think it will work. You really are—"

"Brilliant! Yes, 'tis an affliction to have such genius but I bear it lightly," she said dreamily, pressing her nose against the window-pane. "Now are there any good cartoons on the telly?"

It was two days later before they had an opportunity to deliver the letter. A day's heavy rain had given way to fresh sunny weather with a warm gentle breeze. "I hope Badger doesn't run us the moment we get there," Lisa said as they crossed the meadow, "after your Tarzan exhibition last time!"

There was no sign of Mrs Bradley but the sisters were sitting under the shade of the ash tree. Lily was working on her embroidery again, a sign that she has recovered, Alan thought. He decided not to mention his last visit, but Esme was quick to remind him. "I sincerely hope you've locked up that dog of yours, Albert."

"Don't worry. He won't be here today," Alan reassured her. He had persuaded his mother to take Tatters in the car with her.

"We do have something else, though. A surprise!" Lisa chirped, almost convincing herself of the surprise.

"Oooh," cooed Esme. "We love surprises, don't we, Lily?"

"Mmm!" Lily said, seemingly more intent on her needlework. Lisa took a big breath.

"It's—a letter! From France! It must be from your—we met the postman on the way—and we said we'd take it to you!"

"Oooh!" Esme waved her swollen hands about. "Where is it? Did you hear that, Lily?"

Lily put down her embroidery and said quietly, "It's been so long since he wrote. I do hope nothing is wrong."

"W-would you like me to read it for you?" Alan asked nervously.

"Of course!" they chorused.

Alan breathed more easily and stole a glance at Lisa. She pouted her lower lip and blew a breath of relief upwards.

"Do hurry, Albert," Esme called impatiently. "We've waited so long."

"Sorry!" Alan fumbled with the letter. "Here it is!" He read slowly:

28 June

My dear little roses,

How are you both? I am sorry it has taken so long for me to write but we have been on the move a lot. Just now we have a day's rest in this little French village. It's a sleepy little place—just like Kildavock! You would like it a lot.

How is Kildavock? And how are my little roses? I hope you are being good for Mother and that you are enjoying the summer. It is very warm here in France and as I sit here in the shade I think of you playing and laughing in the paddock as Mother puts Beauty over the jumps. How is Beauty?

(There was a stifled sob from Esme.)

I don't know when I'll get time to see you but please God this war will be all over soon. I will hardly make it home for your birthday but I will think of my little roses wherever I am. Mr Ledwidge sends you his best wishes and looks forward to meeting you. Did Albert get Mr Ledwidge's book all right? I hope he likes it. Give him my regards also.

I must end now as we have to move on. I asked Mr Ledwidge if he had a poem for you and he gave me the enclosed poem which he wrote for his nephew. I send it with my special love for your birthday.

Your loving father,
David.

Alan tried to clear his parched throat and continued:

"*To My Little Nephew Seamas.*

"*I will bring you all the colours*
Of the snail's house when I come,
And shells that you may listen
To a distant ocean's hum.
And from the rainbow's bottom
I will bring you coloured lights

To scare away the banshees
That cry in the nights

"And I will sing you strange songs
Of places far away,
Where little moaning waters
Have wandered wild astray.
Till you shall see the bell flowers
Shaking in the breeze,
Thinking they are ringing them
The short way to the seas.

"When I come back from wand'ring
It's the strange man I'll be,
And first you'll be a bit afraid
To climb upon my knee.
But when you see the rare gifts
I've gathered you, it seems
You'll lean your head upon me
And travel in your dreams."

Alan folded the letter. Esme was whimpering softly.

"Beauty!" she sobbed. "He doesn't know about Beauty and Mother. He doesn't know."

Lily kept fingering a handkerchief and looked into the distance. "I hate war!" she said quietly. "I hate France."

Alan and Lisa looked at each other. Neither could find the right words to say. Esme suddenly stopped whimpering.

"It's a pity he won't be here for our birthday," she said in a thoughtful voice. "He always gives us a treat for our birthday, doesn't he, Lily?"

"Mmm," Lily replied, still looking across the meadow.

"He took us for a picnic in the woods. And we went to a concert." She paused, her eyes sparkling both with tears and the delight of memory.

"And once when we were little, he took us to a circus! That was really wonderful, wasn't it, Lily? And each time we would have to sing for him, wouldn't we, Lily?"

Lily's thoughts were very distant, probably in a sleepy French village. "May I have the letter please, Albert?" she asked, offering her hand.

"Of—of course," Alan stammered. He hadn't expected this. "You will k-keep it safe?" He was thinking of a prying Badger.

"I will keep it in my treasure-box—with all my special things," she nodded.

"We have to go now, don't we, Al—Albert?" Lisa announced in a very determined voice.

"Yes," Alan said, slightly puzzled. We'll see you again—soon," he said, rising off his knees.

"Very soon," Lisa added.

"Thank you for bringing the letter," Esme said softly.

"*'You'll lean your head upon me, and travel in your dreams,'*" Lily whispered, almost in a trance.

There was no point in any further words. Lisa and Alan gave a little wave to each of the twins, turned and made their way across the meadow.

"I don't know whether we did the right thing there," Lisa mused as they sat later in the garden of Glebe House. "I just hope we didn't upset them too much."

"Maybe your letter was too good," Alan suggested.

"Told you I was—"

"Yeh, one of the great undiscovered writers of our time! I just hope Badger doesn't discover you!"

"You mean find the letter? Yeh, I hope Lily has a lock on her treasure-box."

"That's strange!"

"What? A lock on a treasure-box?"

"No. The attic window. I hadn't noticed until now."

"Noticed what?" She followed Alan's gaze upwards.

"Half the window-sill is missing!"

Both were silent for a moment.

"Yeh. Well, it's an old house, isn't it?" Lisa

suggested. "Probably fell off in a storm or something."

Alan continued to stare at the window. He found Lisa's suggestion unconvincing. "There's something weird about that room," he said. "We'll have to get in there."

"Well, not just now," Lisa jumped to her feet. "The wife of my secret love approaches!"

Jane Patterson gave a loud sigh of relief as they drove out the gateway of Glebe House. "For one awful moment I thought your mother was going to come with us!"

"Just as well I reminded her that Granny was coming down to do a big clean-up."

"How is Ste—Mr Patterson?" Lisa enquired, winking at Alan.

"He's fine. At this moment he's either writing tomorrow's sermon or playing with Julie—and, if I know Stephen, it's Julie who's getting the attention, not the sermon!"

"I forgot to thank him—both of you—for the Ledwidge books," Alan said.

"Were they of any use to you?"

"Were they of any use?" Lisa laughed. "Alan has only become a professional poetry-reader and I'm only thinking of becoming a full-time writer!"

They told Jane about Alan's reading of the Ledwidge poems and of the effect Lisa's letter had on the twins.

"You two are incredible!" Jane said, shaking her head in seeming disbelief.

"Do you think we did wrong?" Alan asked.

"No! No! I say that as a compliment! I wouldn't be half as daring—or half as inventive!"

"I just hope Badger doesn't get hold of the letter." Lisa spoke in a concerned tone.

"Badger?"

"Mrs Bradley. That's what the twins call her. Badger!"

Jane laughed heartily but then changed her mood abruptly. "By all accounts she's well named! Did I tell you Stephen called to the house? Parish duties and all that. It's a pretty grim scene. The house is dismal inside. Mrs Brad—Badger runs it like a prison. The old ladies are terrified of her."

"But haven't they got anyone else—any relations?" Alan enquired.

"Not as far as we know. They've outlived them all. And Badger's been with them for donkeys' years. She's a widow. Doesn't seem to have anyone belonging to her either. Like I said— it's pretty grim."

"You mean a Grimm fairy-tale!" Lisa said,

sliding down in her seat.

"Very clever, Lisa," Jane laughed. "Yes, I suppose it is a bit like that really. However, Stephen is making enquiries. Don't worry! The Secret Four will avenge all wrongs!"

They had sped along the dual carriageway and had already reached the outskirts of Dublin. As row upon row of houses flew past, Alan realised how little he had missed the city. Not that he had seen much of it when he lived there—mostly from inside a car, as now—but he realised too how much he loved the fields, the woods, the openness of Kildavock.

"God, wouldn't you just hate to live in a city?" Lisa sighed, as if reading his thoughts.

"It's not all bad," Alan began.

"Oh, I forgot you lived—"

"But the country's best," he continued.

"I second that!" Jane said as she turned into a small well-kept estate. "Now," she said to herself, "second turn right, third house on the left. Number 28."

The car edged slowly around a corner.

"There! Red car in the driveway."

The door was opened by a tall, thin middle-aged woman.

"Mrs Morgan?"

"Yes. Oh, you must be Mrs Patterson."

"Yes. And these are Lisa and Alan."

"The history students!"

"That's right!" Jane stole a wink at two puzzled faces.

"Come in! Come in! Father's in his study."

Canon Grimshaw sat in an armchair, poring over a book with a large magnifying glass. Bookshelves lined three walls of the room. His daughter made the introductions and then excused herself to make tea. "So you're from Kildavock? Ah, I have happy memories of Kildavock and Rathwarren. Spent twenty happy years there. Olive and I—that's my late wife— we loved it there. Lovely people. And tell me, how is it now?"

"Oh, I dare say it hasn't changed all that much—except for a smaller flock!" Jane laughed. "Stephen has four parishes to look after now."

"Four parishes! Goodness me. He must be a busy man!"

"Especially on Sundays! Alan here lives in Glebe House—your old house."

"Does he indeed! And do you like it, Alan?"

"Yes. Very much!"

"He's doing a little historical study of the house," Jane added quickly.

"Oh, good. I like young people to be interested in the past. It's important."

"People say there's a ghost in the attic!" Lisa suggested unexpectedly. Alan glared at her, fearing her interruption might seem too frivolous for the old man.

"Oh, is that story still going?" he chuckled. "Mind you," he added in a more sombre voice, "who knows? We were never in that room."

"It's been blocked off since—goodness me—since..." his voice trailed off

"Since 1917?" Alan wondered, nervously.

"Yes. Yes, I suppose it would be 1917. That was when that awful tragedy happened."

"Tragedy?" Jane probed.

"Yes, that young boy," he mused. "Ach, my memory isn't what it was."

"The boy. Was his name Albert? Albert Dixon?" Alan could feel a dryness creeping up his throat.

"Yes, indeed! My, but you've done quite a lot of research, Albert."

Lisa and Alan looked at each other but neither corrected the old man. To their frustration, Mrs Morgan chose the moment to wheel in a trolley laden with tea, soft drinks and a variety of cakes and buns. While they relished the feast put before them, they had to endure Mrs Morgan's questions about Kildavock before they could resume their probing about Albert Dixon.

"Of course I never really lived in Kildavock. I

had already left home when Father and Mother moved there. The occasional holiday of course. Then I moved to Canada—where I met my husband. But I loved the house—Glebe House."

"Did you ever see the ghost?" Lisa was determined to get the conversation back on her particular rails.

"No! I never did," Mrs Morgan laughed, "but then I never—"

"Got into the room!" Jane picked up the cue. "Your father was telling us it's been blocked up since some awful tragedy happened."

"In 1917," Lisa added.

"Yes, what was that tragedy, Father?" Mrs Morgan had become as interested as the others. Her father leaned back in his armchair and began drumming his fingers on the red velvet of the right arm of the chair.

"Cecil Dixon was a tragic figure," he began. "He belonged to the nineteenth century. Maybe even to the eighteenth, but certainly not the twentieth century. He had a very strict upbringing himself and this was to influence him as a parent. Married rather late in life. His wife bore him one child, Albert, but he was always remote from the child." He paused to take a sip of tea. "Partly his age, I suppose. But partly his attitudes too. He came from an age when children were just about tolerated. And his attitude to things like the Sabbath! His sermons on that are legendary! Hee! He must be turning in his grave at the way the Sabbath is treated nowadays. Gone to the other extreme, totally." Another sip of tea. "But that was the cause of the tragedy. His strict preservation of the Sabbath. Seems the boy—what was his name again?"

"Albert," Alan whispered.

"Albert—was very friendly with two little girls who lived nearby."

"The Thompsons? Lily and Esme?" Alan still could not raise his voice above a whisper.

"Yes. Yes. I remember the Thompsons. I wonder are they still alive."

"They are," Lisa's impatience was evident in her brief reply.

"Hmm. Must be nearly as old as myself now! Anyway, where was I now?" The old man's concentration was clearly fading.

"Albert was friendly with the Thompson girls, Father," Mrs Morgan said, reassuringly.

"Yes. Seems they had a little garden party— to celebrate their birthday." Alan looked at Lisa. "They invited Albert, of course, but old Cecil didn't think that was fitting on the Sabbath so he refused to let the boy go. Seems the boy kicked up quite a rumpus and Reverend Dixon locked him in the attic room."

Alan and Lisa continued to gaze at each other.

"Well, the boy—"

"Albert."

"Albert was quite a determined chap. He was going to get to that party—if it killed him." Again, a sip of tea. "Which indeed it did. He climbed out the window, hoping to shin down the drainpipe, but the window-sill gave way—broke in two. He fell down into the yard. Killed outright."

There was a silence, broken only by the gentle ticking of a clock on the mantelpiece.

"More tea, anybody?" Mrs Morgan said eventually. Heads were shaken but no words were spoken. Canon Grimshaw was visibly tired now, but he completed the story.

"It was a terrible tragedy. Shattered the whole community. Shattered the Dixons too, of course. They never recovered. Never. Lived on for years but they really died that day too. Terrible."

A confusion of images jostled each other in Alan's mind. A boy's face at the attic window. Tom Grehan: "Tell us—have you seen the Glebe Ghost?" The broken window-sill. The tombstone: "Died tragically, August 5th 1917." Alan in the tree. Esme's voice: "We don't want you falling again."

Jane Patterson's voice broke through the confusion "...really must go. Thank you so much, Canon Grimshaw. And thank you, Mrs—"

"It's Ellen."

"Ellen You must come down to see us in Kildavock."

"We'd love to."

Alan shook the old man's hand warmly. "Thank you very much. It's a very sad story." The canon smiled and nodded.

They drove home in silence. Jane Patterson stopped in Newbridge and went into a super-market. "We were supposed to be shopping, remember?" she laughed weakly. Alan and Lisa remained in the car. "What do you think now?" Lisa said, playing with a toy tiger in the back window.

"Don't know. I suppose we knew it was some-thing like this, but when you hear the actual story, it's—"

"Scary," she suggested. He nodded in agree-ment. Alan looked idly out the window. A poster on a nearby lamp-post caught his eye. It was a circus poster, giving details of "exotic acts." Words like "daring", "sensational", "charming" leaped out in garish colour. His eye travelled down to the bottom of the poster where a blank space was left for the venue. In that space, the words

Newbridge 5-6 Aug had been crudely stamped.

His heart fluttered slightly. "No. It's crazy," he said absentmindedly.

"What is?"

"Nothing."

His parents were sitting out on the front lawn when they got home. "Well, did you have a nice time?" his mother asked.

"Yes, we did," Jane said cheerily. "It was an—interesting afternoon. And I must get home to my neglected family now."

"Before you go, we've got a surprise—for Alan, that is!" Alan looked up, slightly startled.

"Michael's got an apartment in Tenerife, through a colleague, for ten days. I've been persuading him to take a break—so we're off next Wednesday! Back the following Sunday week, the sixth of August."

Her face beamed with a mixture of personal delight and expectation of Alan's joy on hearing the news.

"That's great—" Jane began.

"I'm sorry," Alan said quietly, not knowing where to look. "I can't—don't want to go!"

11

The Surprise

hat? I'm not hearing this!" His father, who had been reclining in a deck-chair, a floppy white hat almost entirely covering his face, suddenly sat upright. He gripped the hat fiercely in his hand and glared at Alan. "What do you mean, you don't want to go?"

"I—I just don't want to go, that's all."

"You don't want to go to Tenerife?"

"No."

"You prefer the bogs of Kildavock?"

"I'd prefer to stay here."

"With the bogmen? I've heard it all now—"

"Michael, please—" His wife cast an embarrassed look at Jane and Lisa.

"Please, nothing! This—brat—first of all decides he doesn't want to go to boarding school. Now he decides he doesn't want to go to Tenerife."

He mimicked a childish whingeing voice. "What will it be next?"

"I just don't like—very hot sun," Alan stammered, burrowing a hole in the gravel with his toe. "Remember—I got sick in France," he added more convincingly. "And I'm enjoying the summer here." He threw an appealing glance at Jane Patterson.

"That sounds eminently sensible to me," Jane said brightly.

"Of course." His father glowered at Jane. "Of course we'll cancel the whole thing in deference —in deference to his eminence." He gestured towards Alan in mock salutation and turned to go.

"No, Michael, there's no need for that," his wife said in desperation. "It's a large apartment. Lisa could come too, I'm sure."

Lisa's face brightened but she feigned embarrassment. "Oh no, really, I couldn't—"

"It's not Lisa," Alan interrupted, and then realised he had hurt his friend. "I mean I'd like that but I just can't—don't want to go, that's all."

"That's not all. There's something funny going on here. The whole thing stinks," his father snapped.

"Thanks a lot, friend," Lisa muttered through

gritted teeth. There was a moment's awkward silence. Jane looked at Alan and Lisa and suddenly clapped her hands. "Look! I've got the obvious solution. You two go off to Tenerife, Deirdre. Second honeymoon and all that. And Alan can stay with me!"

"No, we couldn't do that, Jane."

"Of course you could. Alan's no trouble. And he can help out—babysit Julie, do odd jobs. It's only ten days, after all."

"But we've never left him—"

"For heaven's sake, he's a big boy, Deirdre! He won't wander off."

"I don't know..." Deirdre looked at her husband. He looked at Jane, then at Alan.

"Right. We'll do it." He turned and marched into the house.

"Really, Jane, I'm not sure this is a good idea."

"Well, why don't you ask your son about it?" They both turned to Alan.

"It's fine by me—if I'm not in your way."

"Of course you're not. And we can keep an eye on this house as well."

"Well, maybe, but—"

"No buts, it's settled! I really must go now."

"Thanks, Jane. Oh, by the way, Tom Grehan will be in and out of the house anyway. He's going to do a few jobs—especially tackle that attic room."

"Hmm! OK. I'll see you before you go. Bye."

Alan's heart had jumped at his mother's last remark. Jane was gone before he could thank her.

"I'll talk to you later!" his mother said coldly before going into the house.

Lisa scowled at him. "Well, gee, thanks a bunch! A free holiday in Tenerife up in smoke! 'It's not Lisa!'" she taunted. "Me, who never got further than the Isle of Man—on a day-trip! Nobody asked Lisa what she thought. Nobody cares about Lisa. Little Miss Nobody—"

"You know well that's not what I meant. You know why—"

"I'm perfectly sure I don't." She had adopted her haughty tone. She was mellowing.

"You do so—"

"And then you have the audacity to—how can I say this delicately—move into the home of my beloved! Och, I am weary of this world. Methinks I will lay me down and die!"

"Methinks I will too," Alan said, nodding towards the house, from which the sounds of heated argument were coming.

"Nah, they'll get over it! Probably have a great time without you."

"Thanks a lot!"

"And without me! God, when I think of it. *Ten Days in Tenerife*—a story of passion in which the lovely Lisa meets the dark, brooding, lonely stranger who just happens to be a millionaire in need of love following the tragic death of his fiancée—whom I secretly poisoned—"

"Lisa, you'll have to do something with that imagination of yours—"

"Yeh, brilliant, isn't it! Maybe I should write that best-selling novel now: *The Minister and The Maiden.*"

"Ah, come on, Lisa! Enough is enough! Did you hear what Mum said about the attic room? Your grandad's going to clear it out."

"Well, I'm not going to be around when he does. I'm not one for shaking hands with ghosts!"

"Don't be silly! Are you not curious?"

"Not *that* curious, thank you."

"Well, I am—and I'm going to be there when he breaks in!"

"Good luck to you! Listen, I have to go. Here comes Granny Grehan. I'll see you!"

Alice Grehan had come out the side entrance with Alan's mother. He exchanged greetings with Mrs Grehan, who seemed obviously embarrassed by the earlier proceedings, which she must have overheard. His mother ignored him, got into the car and drove Mrs Grehan and Lisa home. Alan called Tatters and went down into the orchard. He climbed onto a low bough of an apple tree and sat there for some time looking at the attic window with its broken sill. An occasional shiver ran down his spine as he imagined a body, arms and legs flailing, fall to its death on the flagstones below.

The evening meal began in an icy silence. When his father reached awkwardly past him to get the pepper, Alan could take it no longer. "I'm—sorry if I sounded ungrateful or anything outside. I wasn't—amn't—meaning to be trouble-some—"

"Hmph. You're making a damn good try at it!" his father mumbled through a mouthful of food.

"I'm not! I just—don't like holidays in the sun, and anyway it would probably be—boring."

"Oh, we're boring now, are we?"

"We did offer to bring Lisa too." His mother broke her silence.

"I know, and I am grateful. And Lisa was too. Honest! But we can have just as much fun here at home."

"Hmph!" was his father's only comment.

"And—there's something we want to do!" He desperately wanted to tell them but he feared they wouldn't understand and might even force him to come to Tenerife.

"Which is?" his mother enquired.

"Save the turf," his father sniggered.

"There's nothing wrong with saving the turf!" Alan snapped.

"Alan! Don't be impertinent to your father!"

"Well, it's true! There is nothing wrong with it! And Tom and Heels—and Lisa—are good fun to be with. You can talk to them—"

"About football and turf," his father's sarcasm was unabated.

"Yes—and other things! Maybe you should try being like him!" He dropped his knife and fork on the table.

"Alan!" his mother shrieked in horror.

"Well, you should! I'm not a baby any more! Why don't you just—just talk to me, like they do?"

"Now listen, mister—"

Alan was choking now and knew he was near to tears, but he was not going to be stopped. "Everything you say is an order! Don't do this! Don't do that! Put your coat on! Eat that up! No-one ever really talks in his house. No-one ever laughs. It's always the same. That's why there's more fun saving the turf!"

His mother opened her mouth to speak but

no sound came. His father responded more
quickly. He shoved his chair back and grabbed
Alan roughly by the arm. "That's enough! Get
up to your room. You ungrateful brat!" The last
word coincided with a stinging slap across the
ear. Alan felt his eyes burning. He shook himself
free of his father's grip and walked slowly out of
the room. As he ascended the stairs he heard his
mother faintly sobbing.

"Please, Dad. I have to! I have to go!" he pleaded,
trying to wriggle free of his father's firm grip.
    "You're going no further than this room!"
    "But I have to bring the Thompson sisters to
a circus in Tenerife! We'll be all right! Tom
Grehan is flying the plane! Please!"
    "I said until you learn to have some manners
you can cool off in here." Holding Alan with one
hand, he turned the key in the gleaming white
door of the attic room with the other.
    "Please, Dad. I can hear the engine of the
plane starting down at the Thompsons'!"
    His father's reply was to bundle him into the
room and turn the key in the lock. He banged on
the door.
    "Doesn't matter," he sobbed. "I'm going anyway.
You can't stop me!" He looked around the attic
room. It was sparsely furnished. A table and

chair stood in the middle of the room but the walls were lined with bookshelves, crammed with copies of the same book: Poems of Francis Ledwidge. *The roar of the plane's engine increased. It was taking off! He ran to the window. It was stuck fast. He shook it fiercely, trying to get either half of it to move up or down. Suddenly the plane appeared, like a giant pre-historic bird over the trees. They were leaving without him! He tugged again. The bottom half of the window gave way. He crawled out onto the window-sill. Why was the sill so big? It stretched out like a runway. The plane was almost overhead. He ran towards it, waving. He could see Tom Grehan at the controls. And Lisa. They both waved cheerily. Esme and Lily each sat at a window smiling, and waving.*

"No! Wait!" he called. His voice was drowned by the noise of the plane, which he could almost touch as it roared over the house. And then there was no more window-sill. He was falling, falling.

"No! Wait!" he screamed. "Wai—it!"

"It's all right, Alan! It's all right, love!" His mother held him in her arms. He was sitting upright on his own bed. He was sweating, yet he felt very cold. "The plane!" he called. "The plane!"

"There's no plane. It was just a bad dream."

He felt so relieved. He flopped back on the pillow and closed his eyes. His mother wiped his brow with a towel.

"There. Feel better now?"

"Yes. Thanks. Sorry."

"It's all right. You frightened the life out of me with that scream. Now cover yourself up and I'll get you a nice supper. OK?"

"OK. Where's Dad?"

"He went for a walk."

Sunday morning passed quietly in Glebe House. Its three occupants managed to keep out of each other's way until Mass time, when Alan's suggestion that he would cycle to Mass was not contested. He met Lisa afterwards. They were about to cycle homewards when to their surprise his father presented them with an ice-cream cone each outside the newsagent's. He had the *Sunday Times* tucked under his arm.

They set off for Glebe House. "It's not easy, you know," Lisa said in an earnest voice.

"What isn't easy?"

"Riding a bike, eating an ice-cream and scratching your nose all at once! Gotcha!" she laughed.

They rode slowly out of the village.

"I've got a wonderful idea," Lisa said, draining

the last of the ice-cream out of the cone. "When your parents go away, why don't you stay in Granny's and I'll stay in the rector's mansion?" He looked at her, startled. "Joke! Joke!" she pleaded. "Gotcha twice!" He blushed and looked quickly away.

"Anyway, I don't think they'll go after last night!" He told her of what had happened at the dinner-table.

"Fair play to you! Even I, cheeky as I am, wouldn't talk like that to my parents."

"If they do go, I've thought of something we might try."

"Is this your turn for a joke?"

"You'll probably think it is."

"Try me."

They stopped at the rusting gate from where they could see the Thompsons' house.

"Promise you won't laugh!"

"Promise."

"There's a circus in Newbridge on the fifth of August—their birthday. Remember how they talked about their father bringing them to the circus when they were little—"

"I don't believe what I'm about to hear—"

"I thought—why don't we bring them to the circus that afternoon?"

"I knew I wouldn't believe—how in the name

of all that's high and holy do you propose to bring them to the circus? On the back carriers of our bikes?"

"I knew you'd make a laugh of it."

"I'm not. I'm just—stupefied as to how you'd do it!"

"What about your grandad's van?"

"What?"

"Lily in the front, Esme in the wheelchair in the back—with us!"

Lisa looked at Alan, then at the house in the distance, then back again at Alan. "You are—unbelievable! That is the most crazy, most weird, most—most brilliantly cool idea I've ever heard!"

"You really think so?"

"Mmmmm! There's only one problem, though."

"Badger?"

"The same."

"We could ask her!"

"But if she said no—"

"We'd be up the Swanee!"

They moved off again. Neither spoke for the rest of the journey but both were deep in thought.

"Let's go down the chute!" Lisa suggested when they reached Glebe House.

They noticed a car outside the Thompsons' house as they crossed the meadow.

"I do believe it is my beloved's carriage! Quiet,

O heart!" Lisa sighed.

"I hope there's nothing wrong," Alan said quickening his step.

"Well, the roses are out in the sun—so maybe he's come to take the Badger away!"

"Some hope!"

"It's Albert and Lisa, Lily," Esme said. "That will cheer you up!"

"Are you not feeling well, Lily?" Lisa asked.

"I'm all right," Lily replied in little more than a whisper.

"She asked Badger when Mother was coming home," Esme explained, "and Badger said there was no point in asking because she wouldn't be home for a long time yet—a long, long time," she added in a trembling voice.

"Never mind!" Alan said, trying hard to sound cheery. "We're working on a surprise for your birthday, aren't we, Lisa?"

"Yes, a—a big surprise!" Lisa said, caught in surprise herself.

"But we can't tell you—'cos it's a surprise!" Alan added.

"A big surprise?" Esme brightened up. "Will we like it?"

"Of course you will. It will be a day to remember!" Lisa said.

"And it's less than two weeks away!" Alan said, looking with concern at Lily. She was fidgeting a lot with her hands. Lisa noticed it also.

"Have you finished your embroidery, Lily?"

"Can't find it. It's lost."

"I think Badger lost it on purpose," Esme said. "She kept saying that Lily was doing it wrong."

Alan and Lisa exchanged glances.

"I like surprises," Lily said suddenly in a much brighter voice.

"Well, you'll certainly like—"

"Mother always makes a surprise cake, doesn't she, Esme?"

"Yes—for our birthday."

"Well, we'll see if—" Lisa was interrupted again by Lily.

"I wonder if Beauty will be better for our birthday. I do hope so. I haven't seen her for ages."

"I remember one cake she made. It was covered in flowers—and you could eat the flowers!" Esme said, her eyes aflame.

"It's time for us to go, Al—bert. Dinner time," Lisa said, shaking her head sideways.

"Y-yes," Alan said. "See you soon. Take care." He looked at Lily. "Take care," he repeated.

"And don't say a word about the surprise!"

"Come on, Albert," Lisa said impatiently.

"Don't worry, Albert," Lily said, smiling faintly. "I'll keep a slice for Beauty. I'll put it in my treasure-box!"

Alan kept looking back as they crossed the meadow. Tears constantly dimmed his view.

"She's going. Lily. She's going!"

"Well, that's pretty obvious," Lisa said. "Her mind is going."

"It's not just her mind. I remember Granny going like that, her mind rambling, her hands fidgeting, just weeks before she—"

"Died." Lisa said the word he didn't want to say.

He nodded, rubbing his eyes. They had reached the chute.

He looked back a last time. "She may not even reach her birthday."

"Personally," Lisa grunted as she struggled upwards, "I would love to wring that Badger's neck!"

Later that evening, when Lisa had gone home, the Pattersons' car came up the driveway. Jane Patterson got out. Alan stayed in the television room. He was embarrassed at the prospect of meeting her again after the scene the previous day. He was also deeply troubled by Lily's appearance. Her fidgeting hands kept appearing on the television screen. Jane Patterson spent at least an hour talking to his parents. He hoped she wouldn't come in to him, but her bright face appeared in the doorway.

"Hi! Can I come in or is there something really exciting on the telly?"

"No—I mean—of course you can come in."

"Well, how are we today?" she asked, curling up on the sofa.

"OK. Well, sort of OK. I—I'm sorry about yesterday—and thanks for offering to—" he said awkwardly, his voice beginning to tremble.

"'Twas nothing. Secret Four—we must stick together and all that. By the way, I saw the twins today!"

"We saw your car outside the house."

"They're ever so cute! And I had a long chat with Mrs Bradley—"

"You mean the Badger. She's evil!" He told her about Lily's missing embroidery.

"She's not really as bad as she's painted, Alan. It's not always easy for her. She's lonely too."

"Lily is dying," he said quietly.

"How do you know that?"

"I just know. Her mind is all confused and she's very restless. My gran was the same."

"Well, maybe. But it doesn't mean—"

"We have to do something for her, for them, for their birthday." He told her of his plan to bring them to the circus.

"What a terrific idea! Crazy, but terrific!"

"Badger's the big problem. How do we get around her?"

"Hmm. That will be a problem all right. Leave it to me. I'll see if I can find a way. And by the way, I've had a long chat with your parents also. They see things a bit better now."

"So they're going—on their own?"

"Yes; and they're quite happy to leave you at the mercy of my cooking! I'm driving them to the airport on Wednesday. Want to come?"

"Yes, please. And—thanks again."

"Look, I'm enjoying all of this." She dropped her voice to a whisper. "Used to be a counsellor before my marriage."

She raised her voice again. "I'm thinking of joining the United Nations now. See you Wednesday!"

12

The Room

 elations improved in Glebe House over the next few days. Whatever Jane had said to his parents had had some effect. His mother reverted to her normal fussiness, packing a large case of clothes for his sojourn at the Pattersons'.

"Mum, I'm only going down the road for ten days."

"Well, you never know. The weather can change suddenly and—"

"I can come back here for clothes."

"But you wouldn't know what's aired and what's not..."

He gave up. She would never change. His father spoke brusquely to him at first, but by the Tuesday evening he had mellowed. "Twenty-eight degrees in Tenerife," he read from the newspaper. "I hope you've bought plenty of sun-cream, Deirdre."

"You'll roast, Dad," Alan laughed.

"Not me! I'm no sun-worshipper like your mother. I shall be sensible and stay in the shade."

"In the shade of the bar!" his mother suggested in the midst of last-minute ironing.

"When is Tom coming?" Alan asked casually.

"Thursday or Friday. Not sure. Whenever the mood is on him, I'd say," his father replied, scanning through the rest of the paper. "Don't you get in his way!"

"I won't. What's he going to do with the attic room?"

"Catch the ghost!" his father laughed.

"I wish you wouldn't go on with that nonsense, Michael," his mother said with some concern. Then in a brighter voice she added, "Your Dad's going to convert the attic room into a high-tech home office: personal computer, fax, telephone—the lot."

"Really?" Alan asked.

"Mmm. He's going to be able to spend more time with his family, aren't you, dear?"

"Hrmph!" His father buried himself further in the newspaper. Alan smiled.

They left for the airport early next morning. His

mother's excitement at the prospect of a holiday in the sun was tempered by her concern that Alan was not coming. Her litany of questions and reminders embarrassed him.

"You promise to eat well? And you'll help out with the Pattersons?—he's very good at washing up, Jane."

"Yes, Mum," he replied through gritted teeth.

"I'm sure he'll survive, Deirdre," Jane Patterson laughed, "and I'll chain him to the sink!" He kissed his mother goodbye. His father pressed paper into his hand. Two ten-pound notes. "Since you're not coming, have a ball in Kildavock!" He ruffled Alan's hair.

"Thanks, Dad. Really, thanks. Have a good time!"

"Now let's hope I don't crash your mum's car while she's away," Jane said as they set off for home. "What will the neighbours say—the Pattersons with two cars!"

Alan laughed but said nothing.

"By the way, I was down with Mrs Bradley again yesterday. I'm getting on fine with her. And don't worry—I'm working on a plan for Saturday week!"

"What about Lily—and Esme?"

"Only saw them briefly. They seemed OK."

He wasn't surprised to see Lisa cycling up to the Pattersons' house next morning. "I thought Alan and I would take Julie for a stroll in the buggy," she said, winking at Alan.

"Oh, good," Jane said. "Stephen's away for the day so I can get some real work done!"

"Damn," Lisa muttered.

"Grandad's going down to your house tomorrow," she said as they wheeled Julie out the gate. "Himself and Heels Dunne. The original ghostbusters!"

"I have to see him about the circus," Alan said. "Do you think he'll do it?"

"Of course he will. He's always on for a bit of divilment. What about Badger?"

"Jane says she's working on her. She's used to handling people. She used to be a counsellor."

"Really? Then I can go to her for advice about my problem?"

"Problem?"

"Yeh. My unrequited love for her husband!"

Alan sat waiting on the steps of Glebe House. Tatters sniffed around among the rosebushes but soon pricked up his ears on hearing the van approaching. He greeted Tom Grehan excitedly but growled at Heels Dunne.

"Sit, Tatters, sit. Sorry!" Alan said.

Heels ignored the dog and proceeded to haul a weighty-looking sack from the back of the van.

"It's for catching the ghost!" Tom whispered loud enough for Heels to hear. "Great man for bagging ghosts, Heels," he laughed.

Heels as usual said little but busied himself in preparation for work.

The sack contained a variety of tools: hammers, saw, drill, jemmy and a long length of wire with electric light attached. They hooked up the light along the narrow stairs to the attic and tackled the cupboard at the top of the stairs. Alan watched as they hammered and prised with the jemmy. The cupboard was fixed both to the wall and the floor but the combined efforts of the men soon dislodged it. They heaved and wrestled to manoeuvre it down to the main landing.

"Begor, they made doors to last in those days, Heels!" Tom said, surveying the stout brown door that confronted them.

"I don't suppose there's a key," Heels muttered. "We'll have to force the lock."

This was not as simple as it sounded. There was much heaving and grunting and the occasional swear from Heels when a screwdriver slipped. "We'd make a poor pair of burglars, Heels!"

"If we were burglars we wouldn't be so careful trying not to scratch the ould door."

At last they heard a snap. The lock had given way.

"Now, lads. Here we go!" Tom chuckled, holding the light aloft. "Have that bag ready, Heels!" He pushed in the door. It creaked—just like a horror film, Alan thought. He followed the two men, his heart beating faster as he stepped over the threshold. The room was larger than he had expected, with a sloping ceiling. The floorboards creaked as they stepped in. They could hear the scuttling of little creatures. Alan's heart was pounding.

"We should have brought the cat with us," Heels whispered.

The light gradually filled the room. It was empty except for a wicker chair near the window. It was the cobwebs that amazed Alan. Huge tangled webs hung everywhere, and when Heels swiped at them they clung to his clothes and sent a shower of dust all about them, causing all three to cough violently.

"Easy, Heels, for God's sake—or we'll all end up as ghosts," Tom choked. "We need air in here badly." He covered his mouth with one hand and tried to open the grimy window. It was stuck fast, but Heels soon removed the nails that held it and opened the top half of the window.

"We need a couple of brushes first," Tom said. "You'd better stay out of here for a while, Alan. The dust is a terror in here." Alan took a long look around the room.

"Are you disappointed there's no ghost?" Tom asked, reading Alan's mind.

"Sort of," Alan laughed.

"Maybe he's just gone on his holidays for a while," Heels suggested.

"Aye, or maybe he's still hiding in one of those cobwebs," Tom added. "Come on, man. There's work to be done."

Lisa arrived some hours later with sandwiches prepared by Mrs Grehan. She made tea for the men while they took a break. "I hope you made the tea good and strong," Tom said, still spluttering from the dust.

"And lots of it," Heels added. "That dust is deadly!"

"No problem," Lisa laughed. "I'll keep filling the pot as quick as ye empty it!"

While the men ate, Lisa and Alan inspected the attic room. Even though it had been fully swept out and the floor dampened, the dust still hung in the air and stung their nostrils. "Maybe there is a ghost still here," Lisa said, looking nervously around. "I mean, the whole point about a ghost is that you can't see him—her—it!"

"Mmm!" Alan replied. He was at the open window, looking across the orchard. "You can see their house from here," he said. "Maybe he—Albert—used to wave to them from here."

"Yeh. And flash torches at night!"

Alan put his head out the window. He looked down at the broken window-sill.

"Careful! We don't want history repeating itself! Sorry! What I mean is—just be careful."

Lisa knelt at the window. "Look!" she said excitedly. On the shutter beside her she had noticed something. She brushed away the grime to reveal the initials *A.D* crudely scratched on the shutter panel. Alan ran his finger along the outline of the initials. He felt himself closer than ever to Albert Dixon.

"Maybe the ghost is in there—behind the shutters!" Lisa said. "Have they looked there?"

"No, but I will."

"In that case I'm off—to make another pot of tea!"

Alan tugged at the shutter knob. It was stuck fast, but with a few jerks it opened. Dust. Nothing but dust and cobwebs. He tried the other shutter. The knob came away in his hand. Damn! He took up the jemmy and prized the shutter open at the top and bottom. At last it opened. Suddenly there was a fluttering sound and a thump from behind the shutter. Alan gave a shriek and fell back. A ghost? A rat? He felt the hair creep up on the back of his neck. He grabbed a brush and, standing as far back from the shutter as he could, he prised it fully open. The dust billowed out in little clouds. There was no more movement. He poked around with the brush at the bottom of the shutter. He felt something solid, and nervously drew it out with the brush. It was a book. Relief swept over him that it was nothing more. He dropped the brush and grabbed the book, shaking and wiping the dust from its dark-green cover. He held it under the light and read:

Songs of the Fields
by
Francis Ledwidge
With an introduction by Lord Dunsany

A cold sweat broke out on his forehead. His hands trembled as he opened the book. The pages were stuck together by damp and one corner had been eaten away. He had to peel the pages away carefully one by one. His heart pounded as he found the title page. In the centre of the page in faded ink, slightly blotched by the damp but clearly legible, was the inscription:

Frank Ledwidge
Christmas 1916, Derry

Alan shook his fingers to stop them trembling. He gently peeled away another page. The whole page was taken up with another inscription written in large, neat childish writing, again blotched in places and very faded here and there. But even to Alan's now misted eyes the message was clear.

19 May 1917
To Albert
Happy Birthday
From Lily and Esme

Lisa was standing behind him, looking over his shoulder. "That's it, isn't it?" she whispered.

He nodded. "They were right. They remembered." His voice croaked. He peeled away a few more pages, then closed the book gently and cradled it in his hands.

They showed the book to Tom and Heels.

"Be the holy!" Heels exclaimed. "Imagine that! It was there for over seventy years."

"And autographed by Ledwidge himself," Tom added. "That would make it worth a few bob!"

"It's worth far more than that to me," Alan said.

Heels went back to work, reciting aloud as he went upstairs:

> *"He shall not hear the bittern cry,*
> *In the wild sky, where he is lain..."*

Tom Grehan was rinsing out mugs at the sink.

"Grandad, Alan has a favour to ask," Lisa said, making a fingers-crossed gesture to Alan.

"You—what? You want me to bring those two old ladies to the circus?" Alan was taken aback at the extent of Tom's amazement. He nodded in reply to the question.

"You must be joking!"

"We're not," Lisa said firmly.

"But—but the shock alone would kill them! Those old dears haven't been out of that house for donkeys' years! And if the shock didn't kill them the noise and excitement of the circus surely would!"

Alan and Lisa remained silent. He had a point: a point they hadn't allowed themselves to consider.

"W-we could have the doctor on stand-by!" Lisa said in desperation.

"You could? And what about Mrs Bradley that looks after them?"

"Jane—Mrs Patterson is working on her," Alan stammered.

"Well, aren't ye the right pair of schemers?" Tom laughed, looking intently at each of them in turn.

"You mean you'll do it?" Lisa asked expectantly.

"I will in me eye! 'Tis more than my life's worth! Now, there's work to be done!" He marched out of the kitchen and up the stairs. Alan and Lisa looked at each other glumly. They went out to the orchard. Alan perched in his favourite tree. Lisa sat below him, aimlessly plucking the grass.

"What do we do now?" she asked.

"Don't know. Forget about the whole thing, I suppose."

"Great Ideas Department!" she sighed.

"He is right, I suppose. We really didn't think it out."

"Yeh. It would have been fun though."

They sat there for a long time, making only an occasional comment. Both were startled by Tom's sudden appearance.

"I've been watching the two of you from the window above. The whole thing is mad but, God help me, I'll do it!"

Lisa sprang up and threw her arms around him. "Oh, Grandad, I love you! You're my most favourite person in the whole world!"

Alan slid down the tree. "Thanks, Tom," he said. "It will be all right. We know it will."

"It's all Heels Dunne's fault!" Tom said, shaking his head in disbelief at his agreement to help them. "He started talking about China, of all places. 'You know, I'd love to go to China,' says he. 'I saw a programme on telly about it once,' says he. 'A fascinating country.' Can you imagine Heels in China? Him that was never further than Dublin in his life! And then he says 'I don't suppose I'll ever get there now, will I? But sure I can dream about it!' So I thought, the circus—that would be the old ladies' China. We'll give it a go!"

"Oh, Grandad!" Lisa gave him a kiss. "I knew you'd do it. Wasn't I just saying that, Alan?" she said, giving him a wink.

"I'll tell you something," Tom said. "Keep the doctor on stand-by. For me, not for them!"

Alan felt like singing out loud as he flew back to the Pattersons' on his bike. He couldn't wait to tell them the good news. Jane was thrilled.

"Now it's all up to me to see to Mrs Bradley!" she chirped with anticipation.

"I don't know," Stephen Patterson said in a sombre voice. "When all this gets out and the rector's wife is found to be one of the conspirators, I'll have to leave the country!" Alan was startled, but then Stephen laughed and ruffled the boy's hair. "But then I'm a conspirator already!" he laughed. "We'll all be deported! Seriously, I'll say a wee prayer it all goes well!'

Alan showed them the Ledwidge book. "You'll have to be careful with that—it's pretty damp and could easily fall apart," Stephen said.

"What my husband is trying to tell you is that he's a book-collector and knows a thing or two about preserving books," Jane added with a knowing smile. "In other words you should leave it in his care for a while!"

"Of course!"

"My!" she said, stroking the dark-green cover of the book, "it's been quite a day for you, Alan."

It had indeed been quite a day.

13

The Circus

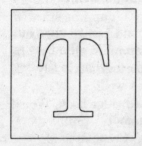he next week dragged by ever so slowly. Although there was plenty to occupy him, Alan's mind was totally fixed on Saturday and the circus. Lisa found every excuse to come down to the Pattersons' house and sigh about her secret love, but to her frustration Alan always seemed to be going somewhere when she arrived. Tom and Heels transformed the attic room in a few days. The walls and ceiling were re-plastered, new skirting board was fitted and electricity was installed.

"Herself will choose the wallpaper when she comes back from the sun," Tom said, surveying the completed work. "The plaster will have to dry out anyway. We can take off for Tenerife now, Heels!"

"Oh, aye," Heels grunted, sweeping the floor

for a last time. "We'll take off for the bog tomorrow and that'll be the height of it. Are ye coming, young fella?"

"To the bog? Yes, please! What are we doing?"

"Bringing it home. Bringing it home!"

He went down the chute on successive days but there was no sign of the twins. "Maybe they're sick," he said to Lisa as they travelled to the bog in Tom's van.

"Maybe!"

"And what if it's lashing rain?"

"It might be!"

"And there's no plans for Badger yet..."

"And there might be an earthquake in Kildavock! God, Alan, would you ever lighten up?"

He couldn't help it. Questions and worries raced around in his head. Maybe a day in the bog would help take his mind off things.

Heels had arrived before them with a tractor and large trailer. The turf was now in a long "reek" alongside the rough roadway into the bog. Alan was amazed at how the once soggy turf had dried out into light sods. There was little for himself and Lisa to do initially as the two men set about loading the trailer with turf-forks. When the trailer was almost full Heels called them. "Let ye get up on top there and there'll be work for ye soon." They clambered on top of the load and enjoyed the brief trip to Lena Ryan's as the trailer wobbled and swayed on the stony road. Lena came to greet them.

"God save ye! I'll be all right for another winter!"

"You will indeed, Lena, and I have two helpers here who'll stack this away for you," Tom replied.

The men unloaded the turf in a pile outside an old outhouse with a rusting roof. "Now," said Tom. "All ye have to do is get the turf into that shed and stack it neatly."

Lisa and Alan looked at each other and shrugged their shoulders. They set to work, while the men returned to the bog. It was fun at first, slinging the sods through the open doorway, but every so often they had to go inside and stack the turf properly. The dust choked them and stung their eyes and they were glad to get out in the sunlight again. They worked steadily through the morning. Heels and Tom passed by with another trailer-load on their way home. They returned in an hour. "Keep it up! Ye've broken the back of it," Tom shouted.

"Thanks a lot," Lisa muttered. "It's my back that's broken." By the time the men returned with another load, the pile outside Lena's shed had been reduced to a little heap. Lena invited all four of them in for tea. Alan sank into an armchair and once again savoured the cool and the quiet of Lena's kitchen. They ate with relish. Only the ticking of an old clock on the mantelpiece broke the silence, as Lena fussed about, offering them soda bread and a variety of delicious cakes and buns. "These are two great workers ye have here," she said at last.

"I think we'll keep them on the payroll all right," Tom said. "What do you think, Heels?"

"I think I'll have that last heel of soda bread if no-one else wants it."

They talked of Lena's mother, of neighbours, living and departed, of the weather. "'Tis a great summer we've had, thanks be to God," Lena said.

"Will the weather stay fine for the next week?" Alan asked tentatively.

"There's not a sign of it breaking, child. My mother used to say, 'The oak before the ash, we'll have a dash—the ash before the oak, we'll have a soak!' The oak came well before the ash this year."

He felt reassured.

"Well, up and at it again, troops," Tom called, "before Heels gets stuck into another loaf of soda bread!"

Alan and Lisa finished their job quickly and spent the rest of the time pottering about Lena's yard and chatting with Lena. She was thrilled with the shedful of turf and pressed a five-pound note into Alan's hand. Alan protested in embarrassment.

"Take it," she said. "'Tisn't much. Ye did a good job—and ye kept a body company."

When the men came with the last tractor-load of the day, they gave the young people the choice of going home on the trailer or in the van. They clambered on top of the turf and sang their way home, waving to everyone they met on the way.

"Good news!" Jane cried excitedly. "I've persuaded Mrs Bradley to go to Dublin for the day on Saturday. I'll leave her to the bus at ten in the morning and I'll collect her at eight in the evening!"

"Great!" Alan exclaimed. "Well done!"

"Mmmm! Rather proud of myself! She took a lot of persuading! Of course I'll be—ahem!—looking after the twins."

Alan breathed a sigh of relief. Everything was in place now. It would work. It had to work.

He woke early on Saturday morning. The sun filtered through a fine mist. "It's going to be a warm day," Jane reassured him over breakfast. "I'll ring if there are any problems. Otherwise I'll see you at two!"

He nodded. "Good luck!"

"Good luck to you too! Victory to the Secret Four!" The morning dragged past. His heart sank when the phone rang, but it wasn't Jane. All morning he had a queasy feeling in his stomach. From one o'clock he waited at the gateway. It was nearly two before the familiar red van appeared around the corner.

"Sorry we're late," Lisa said, "but Grandfather spent ages cleaning out the limousine!"

"Well, it's not normally used as a taxi," Tom argued, "and we have two very important passengers to carry!"

Jane Patterson was sitting outside the front of the house with the twins. Lisa leaped out of the van and handed a box to Jane. "Happy birthday, roses!" she said to the twins.

"Happy birthday!" Alan echoed.

The twins smiled.

"Thank you, Albert," Esme said. "Jane tells us you have a surprise for us."

"Yes, we have," Alan and Lisa chorused. "We're taking you to the circus!"

Esme's face became radiant. "The circus!" she whispered. "The circus! Do you hear that, Lily? We're going to the circus!"

Lily smiled faintly and nodded. "Is Father bringing us?" The others exchanged glances. Jane intervened.

"No, Lily. Your father's not home yet. This is Tom, Lisa's grandfather. Tom will bring you to the circus."

"Oooh," Esme laughed." We're going to the circus!"

They spent the next fifteen minutes helping the twins into the van. Lily's movements were very slow and she had to be helped very gently into the front seat. Tom had to build a makeshift ramp from two planks in order to wheel Esme into the back of the van. She barely fitted into the confined space, her head almost touching the roof. Alan and Lisa climbed in beside her and helped to secure the chair. Jane waved them goodbye.

"I'll have the birthday tea ready when you come back," she called.

Tom drove very slowly, much to the annoyance of one or two irate drivers who could not pass him on the narrow twisty road. The twins were completely happy and smiled their way through the whole journey. The circus was set up on a patch of waste ground just outside the town. The tent was surrounded by an assortment of caravans, trucks and trailers. Tom negotiated a parking place between the tent and a trailer. While Alan bought the tickets, Tom spoke with a man who stood at the entrance to the tent. In between talking to Tom he shouted to the few curious passers-by.

"Roll up! Roll up! Matinee performance starts in ten minutes' time! Circus Europe—in your town today and tomorrow only. Roll up! Roll up!"

He was obviously the ringmaster, although the nearest he got to a uniform was a loud check jacket, a mustard-coloured shirt and a spotted dickey-bow.

"Three adults and two children, please," Alan said. Should be one adult and four children, he thought, but it would take too long to explain. They wheeled Esme out and then helped Lily, who was a little unsteady at first but gradually made use of her stick to walk into the tent unaided.

The ringmaster indicated a chair for Lily in a little open space beside the performers' entrance. They parked Esme's chair beside Lily's. Tom brought two cushions for Lily's chair and Lisa wrapped a blanket around the sisters' legs and draped a shawl around the shoulders of each. "So far, so good," Alan whispered. Lisa responded with a thumbs-up sign. There were less than a hundred people present, mostly children, ranged around a small ring on rickety seating. Their noisy hubbub was suddenly drowned by a blast of raucous martial music from a tape-recorder. The ringmaster leaped into the ring, his agility belying his portly frame, and bellowed into a microphone.

"Ladies and gentlemen, children, welcome to Circus Europe."

One child shouted "Hooray!"

"Thank you! Thank you! We have for your delectation and delight an extravaganza of colour, spectacle and breathtaking magnificence." He paused for acclaim but heard only a ripple of applause accompanied by a few jeers. He continued, slightly subdued.

"So sit back and relax as we begin with the grand parade!" The tape-recorder blared again. It soon became obvious that the parade was not going to be all that grand. Two clowns led the way in a little car that continually backfired. Amid all the din the ringmaster announced each act:

"The hilarious Bozo and Dozo! Samson O'Keeffe, Ireland's strongest man! Madame Zara and her French poodles! From Hungary, Zoltan and Kara, artists on the high-wire! From the mountains of Peru, Chico the llama!"

The audience gradually warmed to the ringmaster's encouragement and gave each act a rousing cheer. Alan watched Lily and Esme's reactions. They smiled and gave each act a little clap. Tom nodded and winked at Alan.

"Chico would be a handy man on the bog!" he shouted in Alan's ear.

The ringmaster continued, often competing unsuccessfully with the taped music. "From Italy, Nico the master of the unicycle!"

Nico struggled desperately to control the unicycle in the long grass. The younger children laughed, assuming it was another clown act. The parade was held up while Chico proceeded to relieve himself for almost a minute, to the delighted uproar of the children and the disgust of Nico, who had to take swift evasive action and do a circuit of the ring in reverse. "The funniest football match you'll ever see, refereed by Charlie the chimp!"

"Quick change by Bozo and Dozo!" Lisa shrieked as the two clowns, now in football gear, tried to retrieve a huge football from a whistle-blowing chimpanzee.

"And concluding our grand parade, the

beautiful Conchita with Black Beauty and White Star!"

An olive-skinned girl in a spangled suit came into the ring standing astride two ponies, one jet-black, the other snow-white.

"Look, Lily! Look!" Esme cried excitedly—"it's Beauty!" Esme clapped her twisted hands as best she could. "Come on, Beauty," she cried. Alan looked anxiously at Lisa. He feared that the excitement might be too much for the twins. The parade completed, the circus proper began. Samson O'Keeffe bent iron bars, split wooden blocks and ran out of the ring carrying Bozo, Dozo and the ringmaster. He returned to cheers, carrying the three, with Zoltan standing on his shoulders and Kara on Zoltan's shoulders. Zoltan and Kara proceeded to balance and do tricks on the "high" wire—a tautly stretched cable about ten feet above the ground.

Circus Europe was by no means the greatest show on earth but the children loved it and, more importantly for Alan, the twins were enraptured.

"Are you enjoying it?" he whispered to Esme during a quiet moment while Madame Zara and her six poodles performed.

"Yes!" Esme nodded vigorously. "It's great fun! Will Beauty be back again?"

"She will. She will!"

Nico fought another losing battle with the grass made even more treacherous by Chico's misbehaviour and left the ring shaking his head furiously.

"And now," the ringmaster announced, "Chico the dancing llama!" He cracked a whip as Chico awkwardly went through a routine to a waltz tempo.

"Poor divil!" Tom said with barely concealed disgust. "I'd love to know how they trained him to do that!"

The embarrassment of Chico's dancing was soon erased by the genuinely funny antics of Charlie the chimp's refereeing of the football match. The children roared with delight. As far as they were concerned, the match could go on all afternoon. Alan and Lisa laughed as loud as anyone and, to their delight, they observed Lily and Esme giggling convulsively.

"And now our final act! Don't forget to tell your friends, ladies and gentlemen. Another wonderful star-spangled performance tonight at eight. Now the high point of our show, the *pièce de résistance*—the lovely, the beautiful Conchita!"

Alan watched the twins as Conchita made her entrance astride Black Beauty and White Star. Esme's face glowed and her eyes danced as she followed every movement the horses made. Lily just smiled in satisfaction, but when Conchita made the horses prance in time with the music, she nodded her head in the same tempo and clapped her hands gently. Alan glanced at Lisa, who was also watching the sisters, while she herself clapped along with the music. Lisa nodded and winked at him. Tom leaned forward towards Alan. "They're not half enjoying this!" he said.

The whole audience burst into a roar of appreciation as Conchita finished her act. As they came out of the ring the two horses stopped beside Lily and Esme. Conchita made the horses bow as the ringmaster announced on the microphone: "Ladies and gentlemen, before you go, we have two very special guests here this afternoon. Their names are Lily and Esme. They are twins and today is their birthday!" He gestured towards the twins and began to sing "Happy Birthday." The whole audience joined in and Conchita brought her two horses prancing around the ring one more time. The twins were overcome. They smiled and nodded regally.

The singing ended. The ringmaster reached over to shake the twins' hands, and when Esme made a surprise announcement the ringmaster brought the microphone to her. "We'd like to sing a song too!"

The frail voice, heavily amplified, stopped almost everyone as they prepared to leave.

"It's for someone far away," Esme added. She began to sing, nervously at first but gaining in confidence as she progressed.

> *"She's watching by the poplars,*
> *Colinette with the sea-blue eyes,*
> *She's watching and longing and waiting*
> *Where the long white roadway lies.*
> *And a song stirs in the silence,*
> *As the wind in the boughs above.*
> *She listens and starts and trembles,*
> *'Tis the first little song of love."*

Lily leaned forward and joined in, her voice even more frail than Esme's. There was an occasional giggle from some children but the audience in the main stood respectfully and listened.

> *"Roses are shining in Picardy,*
> *In the hush of the silver dew,*
> *Roses are flowering in Picardy,*
> *But there's never a rose like you.*
> *And the roses will die with the summertime,*
> *And our roads may be far apart,*
> *But there's one rose that dies not in Picardy!*
> *'Tis the rose that I keep in my heart!"*

There was a momentary pause before the crowd erupted with a great cheer—the biggest cheer of the afternoon. Alan wiped a tear from each eye. "Come on," Tom urged, "we'd better move them out before they're asked for an encore!" The crowd dispersed except for a few curious onlookers who watched the slow process of getting the twins into the van. The ringmaster came to say goodbye.

"How did you know it was their birthday?" Alan asked.

"Your driver put a little word in my ear."

"Thanks for singing 'Happy Birthday' to them."

"No problem! Good for business. I'll have a full house tonight—all looking out for the singing grannies!" He waved to the twins who were now in the van.

"Good luck, girls! I'll have the contracts ready for signing tonight!"

The twins, Esme in particular, bubbled with laughter on the way home.

"Did you see that funny animal do naughties?" Esme giggled. "It was so funny! Then the poor man on the bicycle. Oooh!"

"Beauty was the best," Lily kept saying to herself.

"And the football match—oh, I can't wait to tell Mother!" Esme continued.

"Father will be so pleased to hear Beauty is better," Lily nodded.

Jane came to meet them as the van pulled up. "Well?" she asked.

"Success! Success! Total success!" Lisa laughed.

"Oh, good. I want to hear it all—over tea. I've been thinking of you all afternoon. Come on—you're all invited to the birthday tea!"

They went inside. It was Alan's first time in the Thompsons' house. The dining-room was dark and sombre. It was obvious that neither the furnishings nor furniture had been replaced for many years. Patches of damp stained the heavily patterned brown wallpaper. The carpet was threadbare around the door. Two huge armchairs on either side of the fireplace were sagging and frayed.

Jane had done her best to brighten things up. A fire blazed in the marble fireplace. A candelabrum stood at either end of the table with the flames of five candles dancing in reflection on the china beneath. In the centre stood a beautiful birthday cake decorated on top with two red roses and the words *Happy Birthday, Lily and Esme* inscribed on the top. One tiny candle stood in the middle of the cake.

"My granny sent the cake!" Lisa announced with pride.

"Oooh! It's beautiful," Esme cried. "It's just like the cake Mother makes."

"You can eat the roses," Lisa laughed.

"They're too lovely to eat," Esme said with a shake of her head.

They all recalled the events of the afternoon for Jane, who roared with laughter at the description of the circus. As they ate and laughed, Alan's eye fell on a photograph on the sideboard. It was a faded wedding portrait of a tall, handsome man dressed in army uniform and a beautiful slim woman with long, flowing blonde hair.

Jane led the singing of "Happy Birthday" once again before Tom left to collect Mrs Bradley. Jane cleared the table and left Alan and Lisa with the twins.

"Thank you, Albert—and Lisa," Esme said. "It was a lovely surprise, wasn't it, Lily?" Lily nodded, staring into the fire.

"I'm glad Beauty is better," she said quietly. "Mother will be pleased."

The sisters were visibly tiring. Alan and Lisa withdrew quietly and waited at the front door for Tom's return.

"Good evening!" Mrs Bradley said quite cheerily as she brushed past them into the house.

"My God, she actually smiled!" Lisa said in

disbelief.

"She had a good day too," Tom said as the young people got into the van. "Do you know, she told me she couldn't remember the last time she was in Dublin!"

"So she's actually human!" Lisa laughed.

"I've met worse," Tom replied. "I've met worse."

"Well," Lisa yawned, stretching her arms behind her head, "we did it! They said it couldn't be done, but we did it!"

"Fair play to ye!" Tom said. "You made the day for the two lassies."

"Grehan and McKay, miracle-workers—how does that sound?" Lisa said, turning to Alan in the back of the van.

"You mean McKay and Grehan!" he laughed.

"No—Grehan and McKay sounds better." She looked at Tom. "No," she corrected herself, "Grehan, Grehan and McKay! Isn't that right, Grandad?"

"Sounds more like a firm of solicitors," Tom drawled as the van pulled up at the Pattersons' house. "See you, McKay. Let's do it all again some time, huh?" Lisa said in her best Hollywood accent. Alan surprised her by matching the accent.

"Yeh, lets! That would be a lotta fun. See ya, Grehan!"

14

The End of Summer

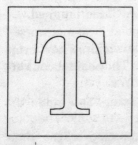he telephone woke Alan
next morning. He looked
at his watch. Eight-thirty.
He sat up, lay back on the pillow and reflected
on the trip to the circus. It couldn't have gone
better. It was worth anything to see the smile on
the twins' faces, the way their eyes lit up when
Black Beauty came into the ring. He smiled as
he remembered how they had surprised everyone
by singing "Roses of Picardy."

Jane was at the door, tears glistening in her
eyes.

"W-what is it?" he asked fearfully. "What's
wrong?"

"It's…Lily. She…she died…during the night…
in her sleep."

Alan felt his body go rigid and cold. He looked
away. "But she couldn't…she was…" He thought

of Tom Grehan's initial warning. Had the excitement of the circus been too much for her? The tears welled up in his eyes. Jane sat beside him and put her arms around him.

"Go on," she whispered. "Have a good cry. And don't worry about Lily. She's happy now—with her Mum and Dad."

He sniffled quietly while she held him.

"I'll have to go over there with Stephen. Poor Mrs Bradley's very upset. Will you—"

"I want to go too," he said, rubbing his nose.

"Well, I need a babysitter," she smiled, handing him a tissue, "but I can get one of the Byrne girls down the road. You'd better get dressed quickly."

There was a strange car outside the Thompsons' house when they arrived. "That will be Dr Cotter," Jane said. Mrs Bradley opened the door. She was very distraught, fidgeting continuously with a handkerchief and speaking in choking sobs. Jane embraced her. "Oh, Mrs Patterson, poor Lily—she looks so happy, smiling she was when I went in. I never thought—till I touched her hand. She was cold as…" She broke down completely. Jane made her sit down. "I'll make a pot of tea," she said. "What about Esme?"

"Dr Cotter's with her. She knows something's wrong."

"You come with me to the kitchen," Jane said, taking her arm.

"Stephen will see Lily."

"I want to see her too," Alan said hoarsely.

"Are you sure?" Jane asked.

He nodded.

He had only seen one dead person before: his Granny. At that time he would go no further than the door, fearful of the waxen features of the body in the bed within. Now he knew no such fear. He followed Stephen Patterson into the darkened room. The curtains allowed only a chink of the strong sunlight into the room. Mrs Bradley was right. Lily's face wore a beautiful, peaceful smile. As he grew accustomed to the reduced light, Alan noticed how her face, white and almost unlined, seemed like that of a younger woman. Stephen Patterson read some prayers quietly at her bedside. Images of summer came back to Alan: the faraway look in Lily's eyes— "I'd like to go to France, to see what it's really like." Alan in the tree—"Albert. Please come down. Remember you don't like heights." "May I have the letter, please? I'll keep it in my treasure-box." Lily's hands embroidering.

He looked at the long, slender hands resting on the counterpane. He reached over and placed his hand on them. They were cold to his touch, like marble. He whispered, "Goodbye, Lily," and left the room.

An ambulance had arrived at the front door. Dr Cotter went upstairs with the ambulancemen. Jane and Mrs Bradley were with Esme in the sitting-room.

"Oh, there you are, Albert," Esme said. "Lily's not well. Did you know that?"

"Y-yes," he stammered.

"She has to go away for a while. How is Beauty?"

"Beauty? Beauty's fine."

"Good! Mother will be upset enough about Lily."

Alan exchanged glances with Jane. A shuffling of feet in the hall outside distracted his attention. Through the partly open door he could see the ambulancemen carrying a stretcher draped with a white sheet. He swallowed hard. He motioned to Jane to follow him out into the hall. There was something he had to know before Dr Cotter left. "You see," he began nervously, "yesterday was the twins' birthday and they kept talking about the circus...so...so we brought them to the circus in Newbridge. They really enjoyed it," he added quickly when he thought he detected a frown on the doctor's face.

"I think what Alan wants to know is if the

trip to the circus might have over-excited Lily," Jane explained. To Alan's relief the frown turned to a smile.

"If you both mean you're worried if you killed the old lady, the verdict is not guilty," he laughed. His bluntness surprised Alan.

"Poor Lily's been hanging on for years with a number of complaints, any of which could have killed her at any time. I'd prefer to think she went when she decided to go. And the way you should look at it, young man, is that you made her last day on earth a very happy one! OK?" Alan nodded.

"Now I have another urgent call. My golfing partner will have an apoplexy at the first tee if I'm not there within five minutes!" He moved to the door. "By the way, Esme's going to need more care from now on. I would suggest a nursing home—maybe Oakleaf in Newbridge." He waved and let himself out before Alan or Jane could respond.

"I'll have to get back to my abandoned child, Alan," Jane said, looking anxiously at her watch. "And we have to collect your parents from the airport this evening—just in case you forgot!"

"I haven't," he smiled, "but if you don't mind I'd like to come back here this evening—to see Esme." He looked at Mrs Bradley. She nodded.

"If that's what you want," Jane said. "Now we must go. Stephen needs a good breakfast before he sets out on his grand tour of the parishes!"

Lisa was sitting on the grassy bank outside the Pattersons' house. "I heard the news but I didn't know what to do," she said.

"There's little to do now," Alan said, "except for Esme. I'm going back up there later on. Want to come?"

"What about Badger?"

"Badger has changed. Or maybe we were too hard on her. I don't know. Anyway she's in bits right now."

"What about your parents? Aren't you going to the airport?"

"No. I decided to go up to Esme. She's a bit confused—well, more confused than usual."

"OK. I'm going up to your house later on with Granny. She's getting the place ready for your folks. I'll go down the chute and ramble over to the Thompsons'. See you."

"Yeh. See you."

Jane dropped him off at the Thompsons' on her way to the airport. "Don't worry," she said. "I'll explain to your Mum and Dad what happened." Esme was resting when he went in. He felt awkward at first with Mrs Bradley. He had not been alone in a confined space with her before. She stood in front of a huge sideboard in the sitting-room opening and closing drawers. Every now and then she gave a despondent sigh.

"Can I...help in any way?" he asked nervously.

"No...no. I'm just looking for...things." She withdrew a bundle of papers, flicked through them and replaced them. "You heard what the doctor says—about Esme?" She surprised him by taking him into her confidence.

"About going into a nursing-home?"

"Yes. He's right, of course. She needs a lot of care. She suffers a lot with arthritis and I'm no nurse."

"What will you do?"

She gave another sigh. "What will I do indeed? What can I do? Mrs Patterson says she may be able to help. She's very kind—a real lady—but not many would have an old...badger...like me."

The word startled Alan.

She smiled weakly at him. "Oh, I know! I suppose I did—do—seem like a badger at times, but I did love those ladies. Really loved them. I just wanted to protect them, that's all. Protect them," she repeated, breaking into a sniffle.

"I'm sorry," she said, blowing her nose into the handkerchief she had carried in her hand all morning. Alan was too embarrassed to say anything.

"They were good to me. Took me in here thirty years ago when my husband was killed. Car accident. They were so kind and not like— like they are now. Ladies. Real ladies." She breathed in sharply.

"Oh! We've been looking for that for years." Her voice rose with delight as she handed Alan a faded photograph in a broken frame. "Look! It's the twins—about six years of age!"

The two little girls sat back to back, heads turned to the camera. They wore identical long white dresses and their blonde curly tresses flowed down over their shoulders. One was smiling, almost giggling, the other stared intently at the camera.

"I bet that's Lily—the serious one," Alan said.

"You're right. Lily was always the more serious one. She used to say, long ago, it was because she was the eldest. She was born a few minutes before Esme, she said!"

Alan found it difficult to realise that he was looking at Esme in the wheelchair, Lily with the stick.

"Talk of the devil," Mrs Bradley said. "That's Esme."

He gazed at the photo for a long time.

When Lisa arrived they wheeled Esme out

into the garden and sat with her. Esme did not seem to be in a talking mood at first but sat looking at hands which she clumsily rubbed together. "Guess what?" Lisa said, chewing a long stem of grass. "The call has come from farthest Wexford! I've got to go home on Saturday."

"Oh!"

"Well, do contain your grief, young man. My delicate nature cannot stand such outbursts of emotion!"

"Sorry! I really will be sorry to see you go."

"Yeh. I know. Kildavock will be real Dullsville without me!"

"It will—honestly! I certainly would have been bored if you hadn't been here."

"Mutual! Now, what do you think of the weather?"

They both laughed.

"Where's Lily?" Esme suddenly asked. "Hasn't she come out yet?"

"Not yet," Alan said, throwing a glance at Lisa.

"I expect she's gone down to the paddock with a sugar-lump for Beauty. Mother's always scolding her for doing that." There was silence for a few minutes. Esme suddenly began giggling.

"What's so funny, little rose?" Lisa asked.

"I was just thinking of that funny animal at the circus doing 'naughties'! We did so enjoy the circus, didn't we, Lily?"

Alan was thrilled to see his parents again. "You look really great," he said, "so tanned and so—relaxed!"

"Told you you should have come," his father teased, ruffling his hair.

"We had a marvellous time," his mother said, "but we were very disappointed you didn't come to meet us at the airport."

"I couldn't—"

"Don't worry! Jane has explained everything. We had a long chat—about lots of things!" She beamed a smile at her husband.

"Why didn't you tell us about your girl-friends?" his father asked jokingly. Then noticing Alan's frown he added quickly, "Joke! Joke! Why didn't you tell us about your—friends?"

"Don't know. There never seemed to be a time. Anyway you would probably have laughed at me."

"Probably," his mother agreed. "But having heard the whole story we're—well, we're rather proud of you, aren't we, Michael?"

"Yes. I still can't believe the bit about the circus, though. I'd love to have been a fly on the trapeze for that!"

"There was no trapeze, Dad. It wasn't that kind of circus!" He entertained them with a detailed account of Circus Europe. He laughed as much as they did at his own memory of the "grand parade."

"Well, God bless Mrs Grehan and her scones. Are there any more of them?" His father went in search of the cake-tin.

"And God bless her tea," his mother added. "The first decent pot of tea I've had since we left."

"So it wasn't all that marvellous a holiday?" Alan laughed.

"Oh, there were compensations, weren't there, dear?" his mother winked at her husband.

"Yes," he mumbled through a mouthful of scone. "I learned how to tango!"

"Which it takes two to do!" his wife purred.

"Mum!" Alan shrieked with embarrassment. "Have you seen your office, Dad?" he asked, trying to change the subject.

His father could not answer, having just popped another scone in his mouth. He raised a finger, leaped out of his chair and bounded up the stairs, closely pursued by his son.

"Wow! They did quite a job in here!" his father said, surveying the bright and airy attic room.

"You should have seen it when they broke in!" Alan laughed. "It was straight out of a horror film!" He told his father about the Ledwidge book.

"So there *was* a ghost!" his father joked.

"Who knows?" Alan said. "Anyway, you won't be the first person to use this room as a study!"

"Which reminds me. About school."

Alan's heart sank. "Your mother and I—and Jane Patterson—have had a long chat about this—"

"I still don't want to go to boarding school, Dad."

"—and we decided to give you a chance at day-school in Newbridge—"

"Oh, Dad!"

"But, in the event of your failure to do well there it will be boarding school for you next year, young man."

"I will! I will! I will do well. Promise!"

"I am also reliably informed that this school is quite near a certain nursing-home, should you wish to drop in occasionally."

"Oh, Dad! You should go on holiday more often!"

"I should, shouldn't I?"

Lily was buried in her parents' grave in the old

cemetery on a misty, humid morning. A small group of people gathered to hear Stephen Patterson read the final prayers over the coffin.

"And God shall wipe away all tears from their eyes..."

Alan looked around at the group. His father (Alan was pleased and surprised at his presence), his mother, Jane Patterson, Tom and Alice Grehan, Lisa, the gravedigger, the undertakers and two or three other people whom he did not know. Mrs Bradley had stayed with Esme.

"...and there shall be no more death, neither sorrow, nor crying, neither shall there be any more pain: for the former things are passed away."

Alan bit his lip as the coffin was lowered into the grave. He mentally whispered goodbye to Lily. Both he and Lisa threw a single rose into the grave. The grave was covered over. Jane made an announcement. "Mrs Bradley would like you all to come back to the Thompsons' house for something to eat."

The group broke up and drifted away. Alan stood at the grave for a few moments until the gravediggers began preparing to fill in the grave. He wandered over to the ruined church and stood in the misty drizzle at Albert Dixon's grave.

"Penny for them," Lisa said.

"Just wondering."

"If Albert has met Lily again?"

"Something like that."

"I often think about it—the after-life and stuff. Do you believe in it?"

"Well, it's what we're told—"

"Yeh, but who ever came back to tell us? It would be an awful let-down if there was nothing —afterwards."

"Yeh," he laughed. "There wouldn't have been any point in being good then!"

"Alan!" His mother was calling from a distance.

"Better go," Lisa said. "Here's to you, Albert. Hope you and Lily are together again. Oh, by the way," she turned to Alan, "you're invited to my farewell party *chez* Grehan next Friday evening."

"Shay Grehan?"

"It's French, means at the Grehan mansion, you twit!"

"Thanks. I'll look up my diary!"

"And then we're going to rip the town of Kildavock apart, kiddo!"

"Really?"

"Yeh, we're going to go wild in Joe Byrne's chipper!" she laughed.

"Race you back to the car!"

Mrs Bradley had worked hard to brighten up the dining-room and provide a salad for those who had attended the funeral. The mourners stood around and chatted quietly over drinks. Mrs Bradley motioned to them to take their seats. As Alan passed her by, she caught his elbow and pressed a parcel into his hand. "It was Lily's. I thought you might like to have it."

"Th-thank you," he stammered in surprise. He was seated between Lisa and Jane at the table. He turned to Jane near the end of the meal. "I owe you a lot," he said.

"For what?" she laughed.

"For everything. Mrs Bradley, Mum and Dad—you know," he said awkwardly.

"Stop blushing, Alan," she whispered. "People will notice! 'Twas nothing. Secret Four—all for one and one for all and all that!"

"That was the Three Musketeers!" he laughed.

"Well, it's about time they became four and allowed women into their ranks!" She winked at Lisa.

The meal was over. His father had rushed away to work. He said goodbye to Mrs Bradley. "Thank you again for this," he said, holding up the parcel. She smiled.

"How is Esme?"

"She's grand. She rests a lot now. She goes

into Oakleaf on Saturday." There was a tremor
in her voice.

"And you?"

"We'll see," she smiled.

"See you Friday, kiddo," Lisa called from Tom's
van.

"Yeh, see you then."

"Shay Grehan's, seven o'clock," she laughed
as the van pulled away.

He went up to his room, Tatters hopping up
the steps behind him. There was a lonely,
empty feeling within him. Everything seemed
to be ending all at once. The dark, oppressive
afternoon didn't help his mood. He sat up on
his bed and opened the parcel. He was amazed
to find that it was a beautiful silver box: a
cigarette box. The initials *D.R.T.* were em-
bossed on the lid. He knew before he opened
it that it was Lily's "treasure box." He opened
it gently to find the rose from Saturday's
birthday cake sitting on top of the other items.
His eyes misted over as he placed the rose on
his bedside table. A neatly folded sheet of
paper came next. It was the "letter" Lisa and
he had written. He slowly removed the remaining items. Little pieces of jewellery mostly,
childish trinkets. In the midst of them he

noticed a tiny badge, circular with a flower motif on top. The badge featured a castle with three turrets and the word *Inniskilling*. He held it tightly in his hand. And then at the bottom of the box, he found a faded piece of paper. It was a poem, obviously torn from a book. He read it with some difficulty.

The Little Cloud

*Take courage—'tis but a little cloud
That soon will pass away.
The hearts that now with grief are bowed
May only grieve today.
Tomorrow, up the azure height
The sun may dart his beam,
And then one joyous burst of light
O'er mount and vale and stream.
When thwarted plans and baffled hopes
Become our only store
And the crushed spirit barely copes
With ills unknown before;
Despond not—yet the tide will turn,
The gales propitious play;
Take courage—'tis a little cloud
That soon will pass away.*

He closed the box and thought of a brighter summer day when puffball clouds sailed across the sky and a young girl in an old woman's body dreamed of sailing to France on a cloud to see what it was really like...